4

# EMILY: SEX AND SENSIBILITY

## *BOOK ONE OF THE WILDE SISTERS*

***By SANDRA MARTON***

# EMILY: SEX AND SENSIBILITY

***BOOK ONE OF THE WILDE SISTERS***

***By SANDRA MARTON***



**Cover art by Croco Designs**

***Sandra Marton*** is an award-winning, USA TODAY bestselling author. She loves to create sexy, gorgeous, complex, tough-on-the-outside but tender-on-the-inside Alpha heroes, and spirited, independent-minded women.

Sandra lives with her husband, who was her childhood sweetheart, in a sun-drenched house surrounded by woods in northern Connecticut.

# CHAPTER ONE

It was Saturday night at the Tune-In Café and the only person inside its dingy walls who wasn't drunk was seriously starting to wish that she were.

Unless you'd had a couple of beers too many, it was hard to endure the raucous laughter and the sharp stench of whiskey. Add in the 1950s décor and the sticky wooden floor and the only thing Emily Wilde—whoops, Emily thought quickly, Emily Madison—wanted was to Tune Out.

Unfortunately, that wasn't an option.

Emily sighed as her fingers flew over the yellowed keys of a battered upright piano.

She worked here.

There wasn't a way in hell she'd have been in the place otherwise. She was the entertainment Thursdays through Sundays and sometimes she still couldn't get her head around that fact. How could she when she'd come east two years ago so she could become a world-class curator at a world-class museum or, at the very least, the buyer for a prestigious art gallery?

Amazing that she'd never stopped to consider that the New York art world had not been holding its breath, just waiting for a twenty-four-year-old Texan with a degree in Mayan pottery.

Talk about planning ahead…

"Right," Emily muttered as she swung into the cheesiest possible arrangement of yet another cheesiest possible tune.

Planning was the problem. Or not planning. In a family of planners, she was the one who would just sort of let life pick her up and carry her along.

The rest of them had dropped from the womb, perfectly organized.

Her father, four-star General John Hamilton Wilde. Her brothers: Jacob, who managed El *Sueño*, the family ranch; Caleb, who headed an elite law firm; Travis, who worked his magic as a financial investor. Even her sisters were on the path to success, Jaimie as a real estate agent with a prestigious international firm, Lissa as a Hollywood chef.

The only Wilde who lay awake nights trying to figure out where she was headed, how she was going to get there and, toughest of all, how she was going to pay the bills en route was the youngest.

"Me," Emily mumbled.

Except, of course, nobody in New York knew she was a Wilde.

Emily had dropped her last name more than a year ago. She'd done it in desperation after she'd realized that, for the first time in her life, being a Wilde was working against her.

In retrospect, she shouldn't have been shocked to discover that in some circles, even in the East, the name was well-known. What was a shocker was that people would assume she was some kind of dilettante who didn't really need a job that paid a living wage…

And what was with her tonight? All of this was ancient history. Why was she reliving it?

She took a quick look at her watch.

Thank God.

It was almost midnight. Her eight-in-the-evening until two-in-the-morning stint was winding down. Soon she'd be out of the Tune-In, and since tomorrow was Monday and she didn't have to work, she could do her usual Monday thing: call up the New York Times on her Mac to catch up with all the exciting things people were doing in Manhattan, and if she ended up in a self-induced pity fest, she could plow through the pint of Ben & Jerry's Heath Bar Crunch she'd hidden in the back of the freezer so she wouldn't be tempted to tuck into it too soon.

Plus, she could permit herself the luxury of wallowing in thoughts of exactly how much she hated, despised and deplored working at the Tune-In and if she'd left out a couple of verbs, it was only because she was too tired to be creative.

And, yes, she knew it was wrong to feel that way.

She should have been grateful to have a job at all. Besides, pounding the time-worn keys at the Tune-In wasn't even the worst job she'd ever had.

That list wasn't just long, it was depressing.

Her one job in the art world had been as a so-called associate at a pricey gallery. That had lasted until the day she'd looked a potential customer in the eye and said she didn't have the slightest idea why anyone would pay one hundred and ninety thousand bucks for a ten-foot-by-twelve-foot canvas of green stripes on a white background.

She'd waited tables in coffee shops and delis where the question wasn't if the boss was going to put the make on you but when.

She'd demonstrated fancy cosmetics at Bloomingdale's and Saks and Barney's—not too bad a gig, really, until her face said "No more" and turned into a giant crimson glob.

Still, when you came down to it, a job was just a job. A means to an end. Yes, the Tune-In was… *grungy* was as good a word as any. So what? This was Manhattan. You never knew when a neighborhood was going to change. The Meatpacking District had once been a place to avoid; the area around the Gowanus Canal had been a bad joke. One of these days, the Tune-In might very well be at the center of some up– and– coming real estate. Actually, the neighborhood had been pretty good years ago, until some fast-cash developer had bought up half the houses and then run out of the money he'd needed to turn them into condos, which explained why a piano bar was in this area at all.

The Tune-In was a holdover. Its customers were holdovers, too. Nobody would deliberately seek it out unless they already knew it was here.

Which was, in a way, a very good thing.

It meant that none of Emily's siblings—and certainly not her father—were likely to wander through the door. As far as they knew, she was working for a private art collector who insisted on remaining anonymous. On the occasions any of her family came through New York, she'd dress up, plaster on a smile and meet them at whatever hotel or restaurant they suggested. Her place, she always said gaily, was being painted. Or the floors were being scraped. Or it was crowded with catalogs and brochures she was searching before buying something new for her employer.

Emily segued into an overblown version of "Hello, Dolly."

Not that she lied to her family, exactly. Or, OK, maybe she did. But they were well–meaning lies; otherwise she'd have to tell them stuff that would upset them. Stuff they didn't need to know. Why tell them she'd dropped her last name in favor of her middle one? Why tell them she lived in a building that, like the Tune-In, was waiting for a real estate revival? Why tell them about her none-too-stellar job?

Being the underachiever in a family of overachievers was hell.

Until she'd come to New York, she'd never lied to *anybody*, but what choice did she have? Her father would go into full command mode if he knew the truth. Her brothers would go crazy. Even Jaimie and Lissa would get into it.

At the very least, they'd all inundate her with advice and cash, and that was not what she wanted.

One way or another, she was going to make it on her own.

Which was why she was here, playing at a bar the Board of Health or at least the Board of Good Taste should have condemned.

Nine weeks ago, she hadn't known the place existed any more than she'd known you could make a living playing piano. Well, not a living, exactly, but you could make enough to get by.

It had happened strictly by accident, the way a lot of things did in New York.

Her roommate, Nola, had invited her to a party. Though they shared an apartment, they were acquaintances more than friends. Emily didn't know a lot of people. Nola knew everybody.

"This party'll be fun," she'd said. "Come on, Em. You need to get out more. Maybe you'll meet a guy."

"Thanks," Emily had said, "but I don't know if I can make it."

Not true.

She'd had nothing to keep her from going, certainly not a date. She'd pretty much given up on New York men. Relationships with them tended to last not much longer than a New York minute, and she wasn't into the latest crazes—one-night hookups or the weirdness of communicating via smartphone, you in one bar and a guy you'd met online in another.

Why party if you didn't want to connect with a man? But Nola had kept urging her to go and at the last minute Emily had thought, why not? At the very least, you could always scrounge something resembling a free meal at a party.

So she went.

The party had been in an old brownstone in her own East Village neighborhood. The apartment was small, the rooms were jammed with people. She didn't see a familiar face, not even Nola's. There wasn't any food aside from a bowl that held what appeared to be potato chip crumbs and a smaller bowl smudged with what she figured had been dip.

After twenty minutes, she'd headed for the door, but the route to it was crowded and instead of getting closer to it, she'd been pushed back and back and back until she'd almost fallen into an old Baldwin upright in a distant corner. To her surprise, a guy was playing it; the noise in the apartment had completely drowned him out.

He'd flashed her a smile. "Hi."

"Hi."

"I don't suppose they've put out any food yet."

"Not even a hot dog," Emily had said, laughing. "I thought I was the only guest who'd noticed."

The piano guy had assured her that he wasn't a guest. He was the entertainment. "Not that anybody noticed that, either," he'd added.

"You mean, you're working?"

"Yeah. Hell of a way to make a buck, isn't it?"

Emily, who had just lost yet another waitressing job, had assured him that playing the piano looked pretty good to her.

"So what do you do?" he'd said.

She'd slumped down on the bench next to him and sighed. "Nothing right now."

"Yeah, that sounds familiar. Well, what *can* you do?"

"Good question. I wish I had an answer."

It was the truth. What, indeed, could she do? She'd grown up on a ranch the size of a small kingdom, and sharing hostessing duties with her sisters at their father's formal dinner parties had been a great learning experience if you were into folding linen napkins into swans, or knowing how to seat people so they wouldn't end up glaring at each other, or being able to carry on polite chitchat in four different languages. She could talk about places in Europe, Asia and South America, thanks to visits she and her sisters had paid to the general.

Because of her otherwise useless degree, she could

also write research papers on esoteric topics so deadly, you'd sooner eat nails than read them, or, conversely, speed read an endless document and boil it down to two cogent paragraphs. She'd long ago developed her own kind of shorthand, but then, that was what being a straight-A student did for you.

Perhaps that was the reason making a buck playing the piano had seemed, at the very least, interesting.

"You play?" the piano player had asked.

Emily had nodded. "Eight years of lessons. You know how that goes. But I'm not a pro like you."

"A pro? Me? I'm an actor. Well, I'm trying to be an actor. I pick up a few bucks playing piano on weekends. Want to play a little?"

He'd segued into "Malaguena." Emily had grinned, put her hands on the keys and joined in.

It turned out that she was no better and no worse than he was.

"Is it hard to get jobs like this?" she'd asked.

The wannabe actor had scribbled a name and number on a scrap of paper. Two days later, Emily had met with his agent. Max Pergozin of Pergozin, Pergozin and Pergozin. She'd auditioned on a piano in Max's office and he'd given her what he called a fake book, a collection of sheet music that contained the melody lines, chords and lyrics of what looked like every song ever written.

"Keep this with you," he'd said. "You can fake your way through any tune."

The next weekend she'd played her first gig.

She'd earned a pittance. Well, union scale but one job added up to a pittance when there was rent to pay, groceries to buy, bills, bills and more bills. Still, it was better than nothing and other gigs had followed, all of them forgettable, none of them steady. When she'd complained, Max had sighed and explained that she was never going to get what he referred to as callbacks until she learned to judge the mood and needs of her audience.

"You play a ladies lunch, they want Cole Porter. You play a wedding rehearsal, they want Elton John. You play an upscale singles hangout, they want Adele."

It might have been good advice, but how would Emily have known? Max had yet to book her into a lunch or a wedding rehearsal or an upscale anything.

She'd told him that, at which point he'd sighed with the resignation of a physics professor explaining addition and subtraction to a five-year-old.

"You got to work your way up, Miss Madison. Right now, the kind of people you play for—they want lively stuff. Big chords. Big runs. Schmaltz. Know what I mean?"

*Schmaltz* was not a word in Emily's North Texas vocabulary.

"No."

"Think Liberace."

"Who?"

Max had rolled his eyes. "Play loud. Play fast. Play big. Dramatic. You get my drift?"

Emily got his drift. And she schmaltzed.

She tossed aside the formal rules a childhood's worth of piano lessons had taught her, added chords, trills and frills, created arpeggios that should not have existed. She never took her foot off the right pedal.

It had worked.

Or, at least, it had led to the Tune-In.

"You'll get lots of experience playing there," Max had assured her.

One look and she'd almost turned around and walked out.

Then she'd reminded herself that playing piano was just a detour on her way to... well, on her way. So she'd taken a deep breath—a big mistake, considering the smell of the place—and told herself that the Tune-In had character.

Right.

Sighing, Emily slid from "Hello, Dolly" to "My Way." Definitely two huge, in-demand current hits, she thought with a mental roll of her eyes.

Why Gus, the owner, wanted somebody to play piano was beyond her.

"A little class," Max had said when she'd expressed surprise. "He keeps hoping the neighborhood's gonna be discovered and he wants to be ready when it is."

Gus was somewhere in his late fifties. Perhaps longevity ran in his family because Emily figured it would take at least another fifty years for his dream to materialize. Still, his optimism, though misplaced, had turned out to be her salvation because aside from occasionally providing musical accompaniment to ancient silent movies that were the passion of a bunch of equally ancient movie buffs in the West Village on Monday nights, this was the only real employment she had.

She tried not to dwell on that, or on what in hell she was doing playing piano anywhere.

Unfortunately, as of late she found herself unable to think of anything else.

*What am I doing here?* she'd find herself musing, and always at the damnedest times.

It was a great question if you were studying existentialism. If you were trying to put food in your belly… not so good.

Besides, that kind of thinking changed nothing. Only she could do that, but how?

"How?" she muttered as she moved into her last hour of ruining more of what had once been perfectly acceptable music and now was pluperfect crap.

It was important to remember that the Tune-In was most of the reason she could pay her bills. Without it, without Nola paying half the rent, she'd be in deep trouble.

Another glance at her watch. It was five after one.

Emily launched into a too loud, too fast, too everything rendition of "New York, New York." She played a lot of old Sinatra stuff. Not that she didn't like Sinatra. She did. Or she had, before this. The problem was that what the Tune-In patrons wanted was strictly Las Vegas Frank. None of the soft ballads, the sophisticated lyrics of Classic Frank.

*So what?* she thought, her lips compressing as she segued from pounding out "New York, New York" to a tinkling rendition of Tony Bennett's "I Left My Heart in San Francisco." "Chicago" would come next. Nothing like ending the night with a tour of the USA and then, mercifully she was finished until next Thursday.

The entry door swung open. Three already lit middle-aged guys entered the Tune-In on a gust of cold, damp wind.

Wonderful.

It was raining. That meant the always late bus would show up even later by the time she headed home. Bad enough to travel at two in the morning, but now she'd have to stand on the corner waiting for who knew how long.

Emily's jaw tightened as she played a glitzy intro to "Chicago."

This was not a good night. None were, not really, but this was stacking up to be bad. The rain. The cold. The fact that not one person had put so much as a dime into the open tip jar she kept on top of the piano. The twenty singles that were already inside it were hers, bait money for people to add a bill or two.

Fat chance.

Not good, no, and she knew that her rapidly deteriorating attitude wasn't helping, but—

"Hey, baby, how you doin'?"

Emily looked up. She saw a stained shirt hanging over a huge belly, and above it, a hand clutching a bottle of beer.

"I'm fine," she said brightly.

"I got somethin' I wanna hear. Noo Yawk, Noo Yawk."

"This is my last set, sir. I don't take requests during my last set."

Gus, her boss, was at her end of the bar polishing glasses with a towel that gave new meaning to the color "gray." He looked at her, eyebrows raised. Emily shrugged and kept playing. Yes, she'd made up the rule on the spot. So what?

"Your last what?"

"My last set. Of tunes. And I'm not accepting requests."

"Thass your job. To play what people wanna hear."

He was right. It was. The correct response to make was *Yes, of course, I'll play that next…*

"I told you, this is my last set. No requests."

"Gus?" the drunk said with indignation. "You hear this?"

Gus put down the glass and the towel and folded his arms over his chest.

"Play what the man wants," he said in a hard voice. "That's what I pay you to do."

He was right. Absolutely right.

"Thass right. Gus pays you to play what I wanna hear."

The drunk grinned. Leered. Pointed his bottle of beer at her for emphasis.

That was when it all went bad.

Maybe somebody jostled his arm. Maybe he was a little unsteady on his feet.

The bottle tilted.

Ice-cold beer poured over Emily's head and straight down the neckline of her dress, her silk dress, one of the few still-decent things in her closet, stuff she wore only for work.

Gasping, she shot to her feet.

"You," she sputtered, "you—you stupid jerk—"

The drunk laughed. Gus shrugged, as if what had happened was the kind of thing she'd just have to put up with.

Later, Emily suspected it was that shrug that put things over the top.

She grabbed the bottle from the drunk's hand. From the weight of it, it was still half-full Good, she thought, and before the idiot had time to stop her, she jammed the neck of the bottle into that big belly, tilted it so that it was pointed down under his belt and into his pants and had the joy of hearing his laughter turn into an almost girlish shriek.

The shriek drew everybody's attention. People turned, stared, saw the stain spreading over the drunk's trousers and laughed.

Unfortunately, Gus wasn't laughing. His face had turned purple. He raised his hand and pointed his finger at Emily.

"OUT!"

The crowd went silent. Emily's heart leaped into her throat.

"Listen," she said quickly, "I didn't mean—"

"Take that 'I'm too good for this place' act of yours and get your ass out the door!"

She stood a little straighter. "If you'd let me explain—"

Gus marched around the side of the bar and stood in front of her. He was big and bald; he stank of sweat and beer. Close up, the finger he pointed at her was the size of a cigar.

"You got a problem understanding English?"

"No. I mean, of course not. I'm just trying to tell you that—"

"Get the fuck outta here! Don't make me say it again."

Emily began to tremble. “I want what you owe me. My pay for Thursday and Friday and Saturday and for to—”

“OUT!”

Her eyes filled with angry tears. Dammit, she would not let anybody in this awful place see her cry! Max could handle the money thing. That was part of his job. Quickly, she bent to the little cubby under the bar where she kept her handbag. When she straightened up, tears were streaming down her face.

“You,” she said, “you are,—you are not a nice man!”

Seconds later, she was on the street, in the rain, in the cold, alone in what that stupid song the drunk had requested referred to as the City That Never Sleeps except it was really the City That Had No Heart.

# CHAPTER TWO

Anger could only last just so long, especially when you walked straight into a moonless, starless, wind-driven rain.

It took Emily less than half a block before reality hit.

What had she done?

Her rent was due Monday. Her half of $1,950 dollars. You could rent a house with a backyard in Wilde's Crossing for that kind of money. Here, what you got was what Realtors called a cozy apartment with charm and potential, meaning it was a fourth-floor walkup the size of a shoe box.

Yes, but it was *her* shoe box. She couldn't afford to lose it.

Her knees went week.

A sob rose in her throat as she reached for a lamppost, wrapped her hand around it and clung to the wet metal for support. How could she have done what she'd just done? Lost her job, especially over something so foolish? She endured far worse things at the Tune-In. Drunks who wanted to warble songs she'd never heard of. Others who figured she was there to be hit on. At least one a night who wanted her to play something that made him sit down and sob.

She'd learned to grit her teeth and survive.

How come she hadn't managed tonight?

The rain was coming down hard. She was beyond wet already; soon, she'd be soaked to the bone. And her jacket was in the bar's back room. How could she have forgotten it?

Emily bit back a groan.

The same way she'd forgotten her tip jar and what a laugh to call it that when what she'd left behind was her own hard-earned money.

She had to go back.

But she couldn't. Pneumonia was a better option. Or hypothermia. Or—or—

A car was coming.

A second's worth of relief morphed directly into panic. A car turning up at this hour back home would have been good news but this wasn't back home. It was a long, deserted street in a very tired part of Manhattan.

The car slowed.

Its headlights flashed over her.

"Don't stop, don't stop, don't stop," Emily whispered.

It didn't. A couple of seconds later, it picked up speed and vanished into the night.

Now what?

She had to stay calm. Calm at all costs. She was a Wilde and maybe she didn't have the Wilde gene for planning and organization and success, but she'd grown up watching her three brother's deal with adversity.

Surely she'd learned something. Yes, she had. Step one? The staying-calm thing. Step two? Be logical.

The cold rain was relentless. Her teeth began to chatter.

It was too late for logic. Logic would have kept her from doing what she'd done to the drunk. It would have meant retrieving her coat and that damned tip jar before walking out.

The only logic now was the realization that she was going to freeze to death unless she drowned first—or got attacked by a local version of Jack the Ripper.

Hell.

That was the thing about not being much of a planner. You ended up with an imagination that worked overtime. Not good. The point was to concentrate on positive things, and there were some.

She had her purse. There were a few dollars in it. Not many. She never carried much cash when she worked at the Tune-In; the neighborhood was too iffy for that. She did have bus fare.

OK.

She gave up her stranglehold on the lamppost and started toward the bus stop sign on the next block. She walked as quickly as she could, considering the height of her go-with-the-silk-dress heels, but there wasn't any rush. The next bus wasn't due for almost half an hour.

Plenty of time to freeze to death.

Plenty of time to try to figure out how to get through the situation.

Would Nola be home tonight? Nola had an active social life. She came and went like a butterfly. How would she take the news that Emily wouldn't be able to meet her half of the rent on Monday?

Dammit.

They'd met a year ago when they were both waitressing at a diner on Tenth Avenue. Nola was a dancer in search of fame on Broadway. They got along well enough and one of the reasons was their unspoken rule about never borrowing money from each other.

Maybe the landlady would agree to extending the date the rent was due.

Right.

Their landlady was a woman of such warmth, charm and all-around graciousness that Nola had dubbed her Miss Hannigan, after the head of the orphanage in *Annie*.

Miracles could happen. Of course they could. Like the miracle of Max's having another job to make up for the one she'd just lost.

She was chilled to the bone. Her teeth had gone from chattering to dancing the tarantella. She'd probably be blue with cold by the time the bus—

What was that? The sound of another engine. Not a car. A truck, perhaps. Or—

The bus!

A big smile swept across Emily's face. Here she'd

been thinking it would take half an hour until—

But the bus was coming too fast. Much too fast and she was still half a block from where it would stop.

She began to run. Oh God! Not easy when you added a wet, pockmarked sidewalk to the height of her heels—

"Ow!"

One heel slipped. Snapped like a twig. Frantic, she kicked off both shoes, snatched them up as the bus roared by. It reached the corner. She heard the sound of the doors opening, then closing.

"No," she yelled, "no, come back!"

The taillights gave a merry twinkle just as she reached the sign post. Then they were swallowed up by the rain.

Panting, gasping for breath, she wrapped her arms around the cold, wet post and pressed her forehead to it.

"Emily Madison Wilde," she whispered, "you are in trouble."

Deep trouble. It wasn't just her imagination that was working overtime. Reality was working overtime. Her pounding heart gave a *yes* vote to the possibility of pneumonia. Of hypothermia.

And only a fool would discount the imminent arrival of Jack the Ripper.

Something moved in the shadowed, boarded-up doorway across the street. A person? A dog? A cat? She hoped it wasn't a dog or a cat; no animal should be outside on a night like this.

On the other hand, she hoped it wasn't a person, either.

That would not be good.

"Be calm," she whispered. "Be logical."

Take a taxi home.

She didn't have the money to pay for one but so what? She had money at home. A couple of hundred dollars, hard-earned, hard-saved, and tucked away for emergencies. Surely this was an emergency.

All she had to do was hail a taxi, but New York taxis did a disappearing act in bad weather. Besides, no self-respecting cab driver would bother cruising this street at this hour. Wait. She had a cell phone. Hooray for something!

Emily fumbled her tiny purse open, grabbed the phone… and watched in disbelief as it tumbled through her numb fingers and landed on the wet sidewalk.

She bent quickly, picked it up. The screen was blank. She pushed buttons, more buttons, endless buttons. She whispered "Please" and "Don't do this" and "Goddammit, turn on!"

Nothing happened.

The miserable thing was dead.

"Dead," she said, and on a rush of fury she tossed it into the deepest puddle in the gutter.

Now what? God, now what…

Emily stiffened.

She'd heard something. A vehicle. A bus? A cab? A car? Let it be a bus or a cab. Not a car. Not a car. Not a car.

It wasn't.

It was a long, black, limousine moving fast, spewing plumes of rainwater behind it, alongside it…

"Shit," Emily shrieked, as a wave of icy water finished the job the drenching the rain had started. She wanted to weep. To scream. To run after the damnable limo and pummel it with her fists.

The limo stopped. Its taillights blazed.

Emily blinked and peered into the night.

The thing was absolutely motionless, a street light glinting off its shiny black exterior.

Then, slowly, it began to back up.

All the fear of the past half hour coalesced into one huge knot in Emily's throat.

She took a quick step back. And another. The limo,

still moving backward, fell in alongside.

It was keeping pace with her.

She stood still.

So did it.

Nothing moved except the raindrops, a thin plume of exhaust from the tailpipe… and Emily's heart, trying to claw its way out of her chest.

Forget Jack the Ripper. What about Ted Bundy? Had he ever collected his victims via limo?

The rear door opened. She glimpsed a big, dimly lighted interior. Dark leather. Dark wood.

She took a quick step back.

"Are you all right?"

The voice was male, slightly accented. Her brain went into creative overdrive. Goodbye, Ted Bundy. Hello, Bela Lugosi.

"*Signorina*? Do you need assistance?"

Scratch Transylvania. The invisible stranger was Italian. Emily fought back a wave of hysterical laughter. Whoa, what a relief.

*"Signorina?"*

"Yes," she said in a voice that sounded like rust. "I mean, yes, I'm all right. No, I don't need assistance. Thank you."

"Are you alone?"

"No," she said quickly. "I—I'm not alone. My—my—my husband went to-to get the c-car."

Great. Chattering teeth added a lot to the illusion of toughness.

"Your husband."

It was not a question but a statement, delivered in a flat, no-nonsense tone that suggested the man knew the lie for what it was.

"Y-yes."

"And where is your car parked?"

"What d-does it matter?"

"I will be happy to drive you to it."

"No!" She swallowed hard. "I m-mean, no th-thank you."

There was a two-beat pause. "*Signorina, per favore*—there is no car. And no husband. You and I both know that, just as we know that you are not convinced of my good intentions."

At least he had that right.

"I assure you, I mean you no harm."

Should she run? The Tune-In was only five minutes away but it was probably closed by now. Besides, she had watched enough Animal Planet to know you never turned your back to a predator.

"That's v-v-very kind of you but—"

"*Cristo,* why do you argue?"

The voice had turned brisk and impatient. What if he stepped out of the… *Ohmygod!* That was exactly what he was doing. A shiny black shoe emerged from the open door, followed by its shiny black mate. Both shoes landed in a puddle. The man muttered something as he unfolded the rest of himself from what her panicked brain now recognized as a Mercedes.

Emily's first impression was that he was big.

No. Wrong word. Not big. Tall. Six two, six three, something like that. Long-legged. And, as she worked her way up the length of him, she saw that he was narrow-hipped, broad-shouldered—and dressed in an impeccably tailored black tux. His face was still in shadow.

Her heart was racing.

Ted Bundy, as envisioned by GQ magazine.

At least she'd meet her end at the hands of a killer who was stylishly-dressed

*"Signorina,"* he said, exactly the way you'd address a crazy person but, dammit, she wasn't a crazy person: she was a resourceful woman who had watched enough reality shows to know what to do in a crisis.

"Stay back!" Quickly, she dug into her minuscule shoulder bag, closed her trembling fingers around a tube of lipstick and held it toward him vertically, one finger pressed to the top. "Stay back or I'll use this pepper spray."

A bark of laughter greeted her announcement. If she hadn't been so terrified, she'd have been insulted.

"Forgive me for laughing," the man said, "and please believe me when I tell you that I can understand your caution. It is, in fact, commendable—but misplaced."

He took a slow step forward. Emily took one back.

"What will it take to convince you that I am not a madman who rides the streets of Manhattan in search of female victims but am rather a man who would not rest easy if he drove off and abandoned you?"

"But I am h-ha-happy to be ab-ab-ab…"

Another step brought him under the glow of the streetlight.

Now she could see his face, and it told her all she needed to know.

The stranger was definitely bent on something terrible.

Only the devil in disguise could be such a hunk of gorgeous, sexy, heart-stoppingly beautiful male.

# CHAPTER THREE

Marco Santini looked at the woman and warned himself not to laugh again.

She was glaring at him like a cornered tigress, still clutching what was obviously a lipstick.

No, he definitely would not laugh.

Besides, the situation was not really amusing. Nothing about his day had been amusing. Why not add this to the list?

The woman was an appalling sight.

Hair plastered to her head, long strands of it obscuring much of her face. Dress pasted to her body. For reasons that made no sense she was also barefoot; her shoes lay near her feet like small, drowned creatures.

His gaze moved back to her face.

She had him pegged as a monster who snatched female victims off the streets.

As far as he was concerned, he was the more likely victim here, first of Jessalyn, who'd been whining over diamond bracelets and raffles gone wrong as the Mercedes rolled through the rain-soaked streets, and now of a situation that showed all the earmarks of deteriorating into a confrontational disaster.

Moments ago, he'd been silently counting down the minutes until Jessalyn was delivered to her door.

All he had to do, he'd told himself, was endure her company a little longer.

If only Charles drove faster…

But he had not suggested it.

Charles had been driving at a reasonable speed considering the weather. Marco knew that. They had been together for a long time and he trusted Charles's judgment even though he knew that if he had been behind the wheel himself, driving his Ferrari…

And then he had warned himself not to think about that.

The very first thing that had gone wrong with his day was that the Ferrari, six months old and the current love of his life, had been stolen straight out of a garage filled with an endless array of high tech security gadgets. Cameras. Motion detectors. Infrared light beams.

"James Bond has nothing on us," the garage manager had said smugly when Marco inspected the place.

Never mind.

One of life's lessons was that you had to deal with what it handed you, and what it had handed him tonight was to find himself a passenger in his chauffeured Mercedes instead of behind the wheel of the Ferrari, with Jessalyn beside him babbling on and on about the Cartier bracelet she had not won at the charity raffle, or rather, the bracelet *he* had not won for her even though he'd bought fifty tickets at a thousand dollars each in a desperate hope of shutting her up.

In fact, when he'd first heard Charles mutter something very un-Charleslike under his breath, he'd half thought his driver had finally become as irritated by her complaints as he was.

Then he'd realized that Charles would never do such a thing. And that he was slowing the limo and peering into his rearview mirror.

"Is there a problem?" Marco had said.

"A woman on the sidewalk, sir. We just splashed the hell out of her. Begging your pardon, Miss Simmons," he'd added quickly.

"Then it's a good thing it's raining," Jessalyn had cooed. Marco had looked at her. Even the unflappable Charles had seemed shocked. "You know. She was wet to begin with."

Her lips had drawn back in a smile that would have looked better on a carp. Botox, Marco had thought grimly, should be banned.

"Charles? Is the woman is all right?"

"Well, sir, she is, as far as I can tell, except that she has no umbrella."

Charles had been born in London. Umbrellas, rainy day or not, were part of his life.

"And she's also alone."

Marco had frowned. Alone, at this hour? Was she a prostitute? No. Not in this godforsaken neighborhood. Customers would be few and far between.

He'd turned in the glove-leather seat and peered through the rear window, but he couldn't see much beyond a lone figure standing on the sidewalk. There was a forlorn look to her. He'd thought of how much he wanted to get home, how much he wanted to avoid spending even a few more minutes in Jessalyn's company, and then he'd huffed out a breath and told Charles to back up.

"Let's see if she needs help."

"Oh, for goodness' sake," Jessalyn had said. "Really, Marco—"

"Back up," he'd repeated, and his mistress had slumped into the corner, folded her arms, crossed her legs, and set one Blahnik-clad foot swinging.

When they were parallel with the woman, Charles had stopped the car.

"Shall I get out and see if she needs assistance, sir?"

Marco had looked through the streaked window. The woman looked half-drowned. She not only had no umbrella, she wasn't wearing a coat or a jacket.

"No need," he'd said, "I'll handle it." He'd opened his door, peered into the rain and asked the woman whether she was all right.

She'd assured him that she was, but any fool could see that she was not. After another useless exchange of questions and answers he'd decided that the only way to deal with the problem was to get out of the car.

Charles had offered him an umbrella but why would he need an umbrella for a conversation that would surely take no more than a minute?

Marco had sighed and stepped outside…

Directly into a puddle.

He'd felt the water seep through the soles of his shoes. Into his socks. And things had quickly gotten worse. How else to describe being held hostage by a tube of lipstick wielded by a woman all alone on a deserted street in the middle of the night, coatless and shoeless in the middle of a rainstorm?

Logic told him to get back in the car and drive away. Honor told him that was out of the question. He had turned his back on many things during his life, but if he'd managed to cling to one principle, it had been honor.

Marco cleared his throat.

"*Signorina.*" He spoke in what he hoped were soothing tones. "I know you are fearful—"

"I have a b-b-black belt in tai chi!"

He considered pointing out that black belts were connected not to tai chi but to tae kwon do and decided against it.

"That is excellent but—"

"And I'm a karate expert!"

*Dio.* This was not going well.

"Truly, I understand your concerns but—"

"Take one more s-s-step and I-I-I'll scream!"

"*Signorina.* If you would simply listen to me—"

"I'll sc-sc-scream so loud, I'll w-w-wake the whole city!"

Marco narrowed his eyes. He had never been a Boy Scout and he had no wish to start winning merit badges at this point in his life.

"A little far-reaching, don't you think?"

"I'm s-s-serious."

"As am I. Besides, this is New York. What good will screaming do?"

Her chin lifted. “Get b-b-back into th-that car or you’ll f-f-find out!”

Interesting. She was wet, alone and obviously terrified but she would not give in to defeat without a fight—and what kind of nonsensical discussion was this? Why were they having a discussion at all?

The wind-driven rain felt like tiny needles beating against his flesh. Soon, he’d be as wet as she was.

A perfect ending to a perfect day.

The stolen Ferrari. The sudden departure of his PA His personal assistants quit with alarming frequency, though he could not understand the reason, but this one had not even had the decency to give notice. What about his trip to Paris in two days? Was he supposed to pluck a name from a hat and hope the winner knew how to do the hundred things it took to keep him from being buried alive in calls, faxes, e-mails, requests and complaints? Was he supposed to hope an untried assistant would be able to sense who to seat beside whom at the sort of dinner he might have to host? What were the odds of finding someone who could get through a casual meeting with clients when the *lingua franca* was not necessarily English?

Then he’d topped things off by attending a charity dinner.

He hated charity dinners. He hated events at which the rich and powerful spent their time showing each other just how rich and powerful they were where raffles for expensive toys could set a man back a small fortune just to keep a woman from whining.

Jessalyn, his mistress, had whined anyway.

His soon-not-to-be mistress. It was a thought he turned to for consolation.

“I s-s-suppose it’s pos-pos-possible your intentions are honorable.”

Marco blinked and focused his gaze on his mission of mercy. His intentions with regard to women had not been honorable since he'd turned seventeen, but he knew what she meant and he wasn't about to make things worse with some small, crude joke that she would surely misunderstand.

Time to try a different approach.

"Good. I am pleased that you understand."

"B-but it d-d-doesn't matter. I'm f-f-fine. Th-th-thank you for stopping but—"

"If you get into my vehicle, we will drive you to your destination."

A flash of panic swept across her face. Brilliant. *Walk into my parlor, said the spider to the fly.*

This was ridiculous. The word *wet* no longer described her. Or him, for that matter, he thought grimly. Rain was dripping from his hair into his eyes. His jacket was taking a soggy beating though it would stand up to the elements far better than whatever she was wearing.

A dress. Silk, most probably.

Silk, it seemed, did not do well in the rain.

It clung to her body, outlining gently curved hips, a slender waist and small, high breasts. Now that he thought about it, he could even see the thrust of her nipples.

They seemed to be very nice nipples, of a size that would welcome a lover's mouth.

"I know wh-what you're thi-thin-thinking."

Heat rushed into his face. "I beg your pardon?"

"You th-think I'm crazy."

One of them was. And yes, it was probably she. In fact, why not? Like most big cities, New York had more than its fair share of the walking wounded.

"Not at all," he said carefully, "but if there is a physician you would like me to contact—"

"I'm not cr-crazy. I just d-d-don't want your heh-heh-heh—"

Jessalyn's angry voice cut through the woman's stammer.

"Jesus H. Christ, Marco," she snarled, "she sounds like Elmer Fudd! Would you give it up?"

The woman's gaze swept past him to the open car door. He cursed under his breath but decided he might be able to use Jessalyn's cold interference to his advantage. He had to do something. That stutter was not a good sign. Unless it was natural, it was an indication of just how cold she really was.

"My date," he said calmly. "Surely that should make you feel safe."

The woman made a chattering sound. A laugh? Well, he couldn't blame her. In today's world, the presence of another woman wasn't a guarantee of anything.

Still, he had to admit that, for once, Jessalyn had said something intelligent. It was ridiculous to stand in a downpour, trying to rescue a woman who didn't want rescuing.

*Va bene.* He was out of ideas and out of patience. One last attempt. After that, she was on her own.

"I am," he said, with what he hoped was a disarming smile, "harmless."

She raised her hand and pushed her hair away from her face, giving him a first clear view of her features.

Nice.

Delicately arched brows. Aristocratic nose. Full mouth. Thickly lashed eyes, light in color. Blue? Green? It was impossible to tell, and what did it matter?

Ending what had become a stalemate was what he wanted.

"Let me amend that," he said, trying to maintain a light touch. "I am completely harmless to puppies, kittens, small children and drowning females."

Her chin rose. "V-v-very amusing."

So much for light touches. He could feel his composure slipping.

"My aim is not to amuse you, *signorina.* It is to

make you see reality."

"*You* try s-s-seeing reality. Go a-a-away!"

"Marco! It's late and I am freezing to death back here with the damned door—"

He reached back, his expression grim, and slammed the door shut.

"This," he said, "is absurd. I have offered assistance. You have refused it. Fine." He dug in his pocket, took out his iPhone and held it out. "Take it. Call someone. Or I'll call someone. The police. An ambulance. *Madre de Dio,* woman!" His voice rose to a roar. "I would not abandon a dog on a night like this."

Or a tigress.

She didn't move.

OK, he decided, *basta.* Enough was enough. Moving fast, he whipped off his jacket. The woman gasped; the silly tube of lipstick fell to the sidewalk as he grabbed her and wrapped the jacket around her. She aimed a fist at his jaw and missed, missed again, and he swung her around and shouted for Charles.

Charles must have been waiting for the call.

He was out of the car in a flash, marching briskly toward Marco, holding a furled black umbrella by his side.

The woman moaned.

"It's an umbrella, dammit," Marco said, tight-lipped. "And this is Charles, my driver. I am going to let go of you. Charles is going to hand you the umbrella. You are going to stand still and listen to me. Do you understand? You will listen. When I am done talking, I will do whatever you ask, including leaving you here on this sidewalk. Yes?"

She hesitated. She was breathing hard, and trembling. He fought back the desire to put his arms around her and draw her into the warmth of his body.

After a few seconds, she gave a quick nod. He took a deep breath, lifted his hands from her shoulders and stepped away.

"Charles," he said softly.

Charles opened the umbrella and held it out. She looked at it as if it were going to detonate, but at last she reached out and snatched it from Charles's hand.

Marco nodded. Step one, he thought, and cleared his throat.

"Charles. The lady does not trust my good Samaritan instincts."

The woman looked at him as if he were certifiable. Maybe he was, or maybe he'd simply pushed things too far to back down now.

"Charles," he said again. "How long have you worked for me?"

"For six years, sir. Seven, come this July."

"And in all that time have you ever known me to do anything illegal?" A tiny silence. Marco swung toward Charles. "Have you?"

"Well, I have seen you drive, sir. The speed limit—"

"Have you ever seen me mug an old lady?"

"No, sir. Certainly not."

"Have I kidnapped anyone?"

"Of course not."

"Are there bodies buried on the terrace around my condo, Charles, or at any of the other homes I own?"

"Absolutely not."

"Am I a thief? A burglar? A swindler? Do I cheat retirees out of their hard-earned savings?"

"No!"

Marco nodded. "And where were we tonight, Charles?"

"At the Hotel Deville, sir."

"For what reason?"

"You attended the mayor's annual charity dinner."

"Dinner, and raffle," Marco said grimly.

"Of course."

"And I was there because?"

"Because you were invited."

"Because?"

"Because you were one of the guests of honor."

"Because?"

"Because you are the founder of the Step-Up Foundation for Boys."

"Does that mean I am a good guy, Charles?"

"It means you believe in charity, sir."

Despite everything, Marco laughed. "Nice phrasing."

"Thank you, sir."

"And what are we doing now?" Marco said his smile fading.

"We are trying to be of assistance to a lady who appears to be in some difficulty."

"And getting soaked to the skin in the process."

"Indeed."

"To the best of your knowledge, Charles, do villains ever permit themselves to be rained on?"

"Not to my knowledge, no, sir."

Marco looked at the woman. The look on her face had changed. That chin was still lifted at a defiant angle, but unless he was imagining things, there was the faintest upward curve to her lips.

"Thank you, Charles. You may return to the car."

His driver walked briskly to the Mercedes and got behind the wheel. Calling Charles his "driver" didn't come close to being accurate. He was also the person who ran Marco's household whether that household was in New York, Rome, London or Brazil.

Right now, he was Marco's final hope.

He had run out of ideas. Either the woman would let him take her away from the rain, the cold and, most of all, the inherent dangers to be found on city streets in the middle of the night, or his attempts at being a Boy Scout were over.

"Last chance," he said quietly. "I'm almost as wet as

you are, but contrary to what seems to be your plan for the evening, I don't intend to get any wetter. Charles and I will take you to your door. Or you can use my phone. Call someone to come for you. Or I will do as you have asked and go away. The choice is yours."

For what seemed forever, she didn't say anything. Then she cleared her throat.

"D-do—do you ha-have a name?"

"Forgive me." Marco closed the last few inches between them. He held out his hand. "I am Marco. Marco Santini."

Emily stared at the stranger's outstretched hand. It was a strong-looking hand, the nails clean and well-cared for. Her brothers had hands like this. Masculine, powerful, just a little work-hardened.

"And you are?"

She drew a long, deep breath.

"Em—Emily."

"Well, Emily, now that we have formally introduced ourselves, may I see you home?"

He smiled.

She wished he hadn't, because he had a devastating smile and a smile didn't mean a thing. For all she knew, Jack the Ripper had had a great smile and what was it people said about Ted Bundy? That he'd been good-looking. Handsome.

Certainly not more handsome than this.

He reached back, his eyes never leaving hers, and opened the rear door. Then he bent down and picked up her shoes.

"Please. Get in."

She hesitated but not for long.

*Oh*, she thought as she stepped inside the Mercedes, *oh, lovely*.

The interior was warm, the immediate relief from the rain glorious. She tried to show some decorum but that was difficult when you were dripping your way across a leather seat toward a woman who looked as if she'd just stepped off the cover of Vogue.

Impeccable hairdo. Impeccable makeup. Impeccable fuchsia silk jacket over impeccable pale pink gown. Stilettos heels, the kind that would never be so unsophisticated as to fall apart in the rain.

"Be careful," the woman snapped, shrinking away from her. "You're dripping all over everything!"

"Sorry! I di-d-didn't mean t-to—"

"This is ridiculous. You should be sitting up front."

Marco Santini's hard, warm thigh pressed against Emily's. The car door slammed shut. She looked at him.

"She might b-b-be right. I mean, I really am awfully w-w-wet."

"You're fine where you are. Charles? Turn up the heat, please." Marco leaned forward and pressed a button. The door to a discretely-designed compartment clicked open; he reached in and took out a bottle of amber-colored liquid and poured a dollop into a crystal glass. "Brandy," he said, holding it out to her. "Take a sip."

Emily eyed it warily. "Thank you, b-b-but—"

Marco rolled his eyes, brought the glass to his lips and drank. "See? Absolutely safe. Go on. It will help."

Their hands brushed as she took the flask from him, lifted it to her mouth and took a drink. Liquid fire swept from the top of her head to her toes.

"Better?"

She nodded.

"This will help even more," he said, withdrawing a small blanket from a drawer under the same compartment.

"I d-d-don't think I'd better. I'll get it all weh-weh-wet."

"Give it to me, then," Jessalyn said coldly. "I'll use it to keep myself from getting all weh-weh-wet."

Marco flashed her a look, shook the blanket open and draped it over Emily.

"Now," he said briskly, "where are we taking you?"

Emily looked at him. He was almost as wet as she was. Drops of rain glittered in his dark hair and on his thick, spiky lashes. His shirt clung to his wide shoulders and broad chest, betraying the shadow of hard, delineated muscle.

She thought about offering to share the blanket with him.

A rush of heat, similar to what she'd experienced when she'd swallowed the mouthful of brandy, went through her.

"Good."

She blinked, looked up, met his gaze.

"You have some color in your face. Now, tell me where you live."

"The E-E-East Village."

"Where in the East Village?"

She hesitated. Marco Santini had, thus far, not given her any reason to doubt that his intentions were honorable, but a false address was only wise. She thought fast, went down a mental list of buildings and streets not too far from hers and came up with one.

"Twenty-two Pascal Street."

Did his eyes narrow just a little? No. Why would they?

"Charles? We want twenty-two Pascal. You do know how to get there, don't you?"

The driver coughed. "Absolutely, Mr. Santini."

"Excellent. We'll take Ms. Simmons home first."

The Impeccable Blonde raised impeccably groomed eyebrows. "Marco, really…"

"Ms. Simmons first," Marco repeated. "And then twenty-two Pascal. Do you have that, Charles?"

"I do, sir," the driver said, and the big Mercedes moved into the night.

****

The Impeccable Blonde lived in an Impeccable Building on Park Avenue.

Charles pulled to the curb, stepped out, opened her door. Marco got out, too; The Impeccable Blonde stepped onto the curb, waited until he joined her and then looped her arm through his. She looked over her shoulder, flashed Emily an icy smile. Then she leaned into Marco as if he were a tree and she were a vine.

"I'll be only a minute," Marco said, but after that little display, Emily doubted it.

Not that what he did was any of her business.

Besides, there was a subway station only a couple of blocks away and the rain had tapered to a drizzle.

She looked at her shoes, lying on the floor. At the blanket, wrapped around her. She was still wearing her rescuer's jacket but the blanket would be enough…

"Mr. Santini would never forgive me, Miss."

She blinked, looked up, met Charles's steady eyes in the mirror.

"Would you really try to stop me?"

"I'm trying to do that right now, Miss, by talking you out of leaving."

"Just that?"

Charles smiled. "Mr. Santini is a man of honor. He wouldn't approve of anything more. You don't have to worry about—"

The door opened. "What doesn't she have to worry about?" Marco said as he got into the car.

"About getting to twenty-two Pascal," Charles said smoothly. "I know precisely where it is."

"Indeed. So do I. And we both know that it isn't where the lady lives."

Emily stared at him. "Why would you say that?"

"Because it is a landmark building that has just undergone extensive renovations. It took the builder five hard years to gain the city's approval."

She sank back in the seat. "Oh."

"Oh, indeed. Now, *prego*, where do you really live?

She told him and ten minutes later they reached her slightly decrepit building. Emily shrugged off the blanket and stepped onto the sidewalk before either Marco or his driver had moved.

"Well," she said briskly, "thank you for—"

Marco held out her shoes. "You forgot these."

"Oh." She reached for them but he shook his head as he got out of the car.

"I'll carry them for you."

"No. I mean, you don't have to."

"A gentleman always escorts a lady to her door."

Was he making fun of her? She couldn't tell, not from his voice or from his expression.

"Really, that isn't—"

"And I can collect my jacket at the same time."

"Your jacket. Sorry. I forgot—"

"No, keep it on. You can give it to me after we get to your apartment."

"Really, Mr. Santini—"

"It's Marco." His hand closed on her elbow. "What floor?"

"The fourth. And it's a walk-up."

"I expected nothing less," he said dryly. "Keys."

"Excuse me?"

"Your keys I am assuming the front door is locked."

It was, and how could she balk now after he'd driven her all the way home? Emily dug the keys from her purse and handed them over.

The stairs were narrow; they climbed them single file, he in back of her. At the fourth floor landing, she swung toward him.

"Thank you for everything."

"You're welcome. Which door is yours?"

"Mr. Santini—"

"Marco."

"Marco. It isn't necessary to—" She took a breath.

"That one." He moved past her, unlocked her door, then took her hand, pressed the keys into it and folded her fingers over them. She looked at her hand, then at him. A wash of pale pink rose in her face. "I'm not going to ask you in."

He laughed softly. "I didn't think you would."

"Good. Fine. Because—"

"Because you think, now he will demand recompense."

Emily blushed. "No. I just—"

"Yet, you must admit, you do owe me something."

She stiffened.

"It was very kind of you to bring me home but if you think that entitles you to—"

"It does," he said solemnly.

"No. It does not. I am not about to—"

"What were you doing on that street corner?"

"Huh?"

"That is the cost of my assistance. I want to know what happened to you tonight."

Emily stared at him. "That's it?"

"That's it."

"Well…" She caught her bottom lip between her teeth. "I was fired."

"You were fired?"

"Uh-huh."

"From what?"

She could hear the bewilderment in his voice, see it in his eyes. Who could blame him? It sounded unreal; if their positions had been reversed, she wouldn't have believed the story either.

"From a bar. The Tune-In Café. It's a couple of blocks from where you found me."

His eyebrows rose. "Are you saying that you are a bartender?"

"A bar…?" She laughed. It was, he noticed a very nice laugh. It went with her eyes—light blue, he could see now, in the faint glow of light in the hall. "No," she said, "I play piano."

"Ah. A pianist."

"Pianists play at Carnegie Hall. Piano players play at places like the Tune-In."

She was smiling. He smiled back. His tigress had a nice way about her. She was very pretty, too. Not the type of pretty he generally saw. Her face was bare of makeup. Her hair was the color of gold. The heat of the car had dried it and it fell down her back in a drift of soft curls.

He wanted to reach out and touch one of them. See if it would wrap around his finger. He couldn't remember the last time he'd touched a woman's hair that had not been sprayed, shellacked or cemented into place.

"And what did you do to deserve being fired?"

She hesitated. "You wouldn't understand."

He folded his arms over his chest. It was either that or succumb to the desire to play with one of those curls, and he suspected that would not be a good idea.

"Try me."

Her voice took on a defensive edge. "A guy asked me to play a tune. I refused."

"Was it something you didn't know?"

"I knew it, all right. It was that old Sinatra thing. "New York, New York."

"But aren't requests part of a pianist's—*scusi*—a piano player's job?"

Why had she let the conversation get this far? Talking about what she'd done only emphasized the stupidity of it.

"Yes."

"So, your boss told you to get out because you wouldn't play the tune?"

"Not exactly. See, the guy who'd asked me to play that song was drunk."

His face seemed to darken. "Did he do something to you? Did he touch you?"

"No," she said quickly, "nothing like that. He was just drunk. And he had an open bottle of beer in his hand. He pointed it at me."

"And?"

"And..." She ran the tip of her tongue over her bottom lip. "It's too embarrassing."

Marco put his finger lightly under her chin, lifted her face until their eyes met. "Tell me."

"The beer spilled. Over me."

Marco said something in Italian. Italian was one of the four languages Emily could speak and what he'd said wasn't very nice but it was well-deserved. She thought of telling him that, but why prolong this conversation?

"So I grabbed the bottle from him." She paused. "There was still beer left in it."

"And?" he said again.

She gave a little shrug. "And I shoved it upside down into the top of his pants and all the beer poured out and—"

Marco snorted.

"Don't laugh at me! It isn't funny! If I hadn't done such a—such a dumb, impetuous thing—"

Laughter rumbled from his chest

"I wish I had been there to see it!"

She blinked. "You do?"

"Trust me, Emily. The world is filled with fools who could use a good dousing in beer."

His smile, his laughter were impossible to resist. Emily laughed, too.

"My boss was horrified."

"What is the name of this place again? I'll pay him a visit. He should not have fired you. He should have stood by you."

"No. Please, never mind. He'd only give you a hard time."

She looked so serious, it made him want to smile,

but what he most wanted was to give in to temptation and take one of those curls between his fingers.

"I am not afraid of hard times, Emily." To hell with it. He not only smiled, he reached out and caught hold of a curl. It felt like silk. "And you are very brave."

She smiled. "Not without a tube of lipstick in my hand."

"I mean it. You put a drunken fool in his place, stood up to a stranger, withstood a monsoon…" His gaze fell to her lips, rose to her eyes. "And you risked everything by accepting his offer of a ride home. A tigress, indeed."

Silly, she knew that his praise should send a rush of warmth through her.

"Thank you."

"It is the truth." He drew the curl to its full length; let it wind itself back around his finger. "What happens now? Will it be difficult to find another job?"

"Oh, no, not at all," Emily said airily. How could she ruin her rescuer's view of her as a tigress by admitting the truth? "I have a wonderful agent. He won't have any difficulty getting me something even better."

"Good. Because if you were to have a problem, I would be happy to help." He smiled. "I'm afraid I could not offer you employment playing the piano but I have contacts…"

"Thanks, but I'm fine."

His smile tilted. "Yes," he said. "You most certainly are."

Suddenly, the air seemed thick. Words had more than one meaning. Emily could hear her pulse beating in her ears as Marco slid his hands to her shoulders.

Then he let go of her and she took a step back.

"Well," she said, "good night."

"Good night."

"Thank you again. For everything."

"It was my pleasure."

"But I spoiled your evening."

"On the contrary. You were a charming note in an otherwise very long and dull night."

"Yes, but your friend—Miss Simmons…"

He shrugged.

"It's unfortunate you were subjected to that. What you saw…" Another lift of those wide shoulders. "Our—situation had run its natural course. Such things always come to an end."

He said it almost casually. Emily wasn't surprised. Her brothers were all happily married now but she remembered their bachelor days. She and her sisters used to joke that you needed a calculator to keep track of the women who floated in and out of their lives, and she certainly felt no sympathy for Jessalyn Simmons. Still, his easy dismissal of the relationship was somehow troubling.

"I only wish I had not frightened you."

"You didn't. I mean, not deliberately. Stopping for me, giving me your jacket… oh, your jacket! I almost forgot—"

She began to take it off. He reached for it, grasped the lapels and brought them together.

"Keep it."

"No. I couldn't. Really, I—"

"Keep it," he said his voice suddenly low and rough.

She looked up, met his gaze. The world seemed to drop away.

"Keep the jacket," he said, and he bent his head and kissed her.

It was the softest of kisses. Just the gentle brush of his lips over hers. For an endless moment, Emily did nothing. Then she sighed and her lips softened and parted under the delicious feel of his.

He felt his body take fire.

In a heartbeat, she was in his arms, rising on her toes as she strained toward him. He groaned, took the kiss deeper, heard her moan as her hands rose, clutched his arms, his shoulders.

*Now*, he thought, with a ferocity that drove out everything else. All he had to do was whisper to her, follow her inside the dark apartment. She would lose herself in his kisses, in his caresses. He would undress her, see that lovely body the rain had so temptingly hinted at...

*Cristo!*

What in hell was he thinking? She was brave but she was also naïve. He had asked for her trust; she had given it. Was this how he would repay her?

Marco tore his mouth from hers. He drew her hands to her sides and waited until, at last, her lashes lifted and her eyes, blurred and the color of the sea, met his.

"Forgive me," he said gruffly, and then he was gone.

# CHAPTER FOUR

According to the lighted numbers on his bedside radio, it was 3:58 in the morning.

Marco was still wide awake.

He'd tossed and turned and all he'd succeeded in doing was making a Gordian knot of the bed linens. When the numbers on the face of the clock radio hit four, he mouthed an oath and gave it up.

His triplex penthouse was silent. Charles's rooms were in the staff wing on the lower level; the housekeeper wouldn't be in until seven. Good. He really wasn't in the mood to attempt civil conversation right now.

He rose from the bed, pulled on a pair of sweatpants and a sweatshirt, and then went down the curved wood-and-glass staircase and along the hall to the kitchen. The espresso machine was at the ready; he made a quick cup of dark, strong coffee, opened the French doors that led to the terrace and stepped outside.

It was only September but surprisingly cold, the wind moaning as it whipped through the Wollemi pines and Sicilian olive trees that formed a small forest in one curving arm of the terrace.

He'd been far too busy to involve himself directly in the furnishing of the condo itself or of the terrace. He'd instructed his designer to use lots of glass and pale woods; she had worked on the plans for weeks and then presented computerized photos for Marco's approval. He'd gone through them quickly, saying things like "Good" and "Fine" and "Very nice" until he came to the plans for the terrace.

The designer showed an arrangement of comfortable furniture along its two levels; a cooking center on the main level, which Marco had rightly suspected he would never find time to use, and a handsome reflecting pool.

There were plantings of shrubs, flowers and succulents.

And, for the first time, Marco had asked for something specific.

He said he wanted trees.

Real trees, not the botanical hybrids that a man of his height would dwarf.

His designer as well as the landscape architect had warned him that it would be difficult to find trees that could endure the wind. There were days the air was perfectly still, of course, but when you were up this high, exposed to the elements, a stiff wind could strip away the leaves that trees needed to survive.

Marco had remained unmoved. He wanted trees—and he got them. Olive trees from Sicily. Woolemi pines from Australia. Tough trees that would not succumb to the worst the world might toss at them.

According to a woman he'd dated a couple of years ago, the trees were subconscious representations of his own survival.

Marco took a mouthful of coffee.

"These trees are you," she'd told him. "They're tough. Strong. They can take a beating from life; they're impervious to what happens once you climb this high."

He'd scoffed at such foolishness.

"Psychological game playing," he'd told her. "I simply like trees."

"Exactly. And the reason you like them is because they remind you of yourself."

He'd laughed and said that he was nothing like the trees.

"Yes," she'd said, "you are—but there's one big difference. The trees know that despite their tough exteriors, they require care. TLC."

"What?"

"TLC. Tender loving care."

"I know what the letters mean," he'd replied, "and it's pure nonsense. These trees don't 'know' anything.

And what they require are only life's basics. That's one of the reasons I chose them."

He could still remember the way she'd looked at him.

"Living things need more than that to flourish. Even these trees. Even you."

Marco sipped at the coffee.

He'd ended the foolish conversation by taking her back to bed but their affair had not lasted very long after that.

"I want more," she'd told him, and they'd both known she hadn't meant more jewelry or clothes or other gifts, just as they'd both known that he didn't have more to give.

He had, once.

A decade ago.

In two short, amazing years he'd made his first million, made his second, his third and fourth. He'd also met a woman, lost his heart to her, or so he'd thought, and asked her to marry him.

At first, things were fine. Coming home to someone at the end of a long day was new to him. He liked the feeling. He liked having someone to care about.

A business opportunity came along.

It was risky. If he invested in it, he could make millions. He could also lose almost everything he had. He didn't think that would happen, but when you took risk, there was always that possibility. Still, he was young. Hardworking. And he had a woman standing beside him who loved him.

Wrong.

He told his wife about the investment. He wanted to hear her opinion. And she gave it.

If he lost everything, she said calmly, he would also lose her. What about love? he said, and she said, What about it?

The divorce was quick, the settlement her lawyers

got out of him substantial.

The last time he saw her, he'd heard himself ask the question he'd sworn he would not ask.

"Was it all a lie?" he'd said.

She'd smiled, touched his shoulder.

"Not the sex."

It had been a hard lesson. An awful lesson, but he had learned it well.

He was not a man meant for love. He had raised himself out of poverty, alone. He had created a life for himself, alone. He had become the man he was, alone.

He needed no one. He never would.

The trees bent to a gust of wind. Marco shivered.

Why was he thinking about these things? More to the point, why couldn't he sleep?

No, it had not been a good day. The Ferrari. His PA. Jessalyn. Annoyances, all of them, but he'd had worse days, especially years ago, days when he had not known where he would get his next meal, when his dreams of success had seemed more distant than the stars.

Nothing that had happened today came close to that.

And yet here he was, standing on his terrace at four-something in the morning, facing another long day ahead, needing sleep and knowing it would not come.

For what reason?

He was not a man given to insomnia. He worked hard, played hard. Literally. He had a workout room on the lower level of the penthouse. He played racquetball. Soccer. American football. He had little time for those things, of course, but when he did, he gave no quarter and expected none. And he slept soundly.

So, what was he doing out here at this hour?

He exhaled heavily, then brought the cup of espresso to his mouth and swallowed the last of the bitter liquid.

He knew the answer.

It was Emily. A rain-soaked waif who had turned out to be tough and determined was in his head.

His lips curved in a smile.

Not many people had the balls to take him on. The fact was, Charles was the only one who ever did and Charles did it with so much tact, it was hard to know he was doing it.

But Emily had stood up to him without hesitation and even though she'd eventually accepted his help, she had been about as impressed by him and his car and the indications of his obvious wealth as these trees were impressed by the city sprawled at their feet.

And that kiss…

He imagined he could still taste the sweetness of her lips, feel the softness of her against him.

What would she have been like in bed?

Like her kiss. Sweet. Tender. But with fire blazing underneath.

His body hardened at the thought.

*Dio,* was that what was keeping him awake? Sexual frustration? It didn't seem possible. Besides, he'd done the right thing, walking away, not taking things further.

Hadn't he?

Of course. A woman like Emily had no place in his world. In his life… and what in hell did that mean? He didn't even know her last name; he hadn't asked for her phone number and here he was deciding she wouldn't fit into his life.

He was a crazy man.

He was a man in desperate need of sleep.

Or activity.

Marco strode back into the penthouse, dumped the cup into the sink, went to his workout room and spent an hour lifting weights. The sky had lightened to a pale gray by the time he was done but he fell into bed, and sleep took pity on him and swallowed him up for one mindless, restful hour.

****

The alarm went off at seven. Marco rose, shaved, showered, dressed in a dark navy suit, white shirt, burgundy tie.

His housekeeper was already in the kitchen and she knew his routine. Orange juice. Half a toasted bagel. A double espresso. Charles was at the table, drinking his usual mug of Earl Grey.

"Ready, sir?"

Marco would have preferred his Ferrari. No point in thinking about that.

"*Si.* I am ready."

Traffic was mercifully swift-moving. Charles pulled the Mercedes to the curb in front of the MS Enterprises building. He knew better than to open the door for his employer.

"See you at six, sir."

Marco nodded, stepped from the car and walked briskly toward the building entrance.

A watery sun was in the sky. The air was crisp. He felt surprisingly good for a man who'd had one hour of sleep.

Perhaps it was because he'd made peace with the Emily incident.

She was attractive and he admired her spirit, but his attraction to her hadn't been real. It had been the natural follow-through to the entire situation. Woman in need, man riding to the rescue, a modern-day version of playing Sir Galahad when he was far more accustomed to being viewed as a heartless marauder.

And then there'd been the sharp contrast between Emily and Jessalyn.

Marco quickened his pace as he crossed the enormous lobby of MS Enterprises.

Emily was not the kind of woman he normally dealt with. She was most certainly not the kind he wanted to deal with.

Bottom line? He was glad he'd helped her but that

was the end of it.

He strode past the lobby reception desk. The clerk behind it sprang to his feet and all but clicked his heels.

"Good morning, Mr. Santini."

Marco growled a good morning in return. He considered pausing long enough to say that a simple greeting was sufficient, that standing at attention was not necessary, but he'd made the same little speech before and it had gotten him nowhere.

The elevator operator—not really an operator but a security guy—did the same thing. Straightened up and damn near saluted.

"Good morning, sir."

Marco nodded, and also thought about telling him, once again, that such formality was not necessary, but the elevator doors whisked open and he stepped inside.

He didn't like being treated like a potentate. Why would he?

The car stopped at the fiftieth floor. The executive level, fronted by a big glass desk and a receptionist.

"Good morning, Mr. Santini…"

"You are not to rise to your feet," Marco snapped.

The woman looked bewildered, and rightly so. She, at least, had taken him at his word after the millionth time he'd told her to remain seated when he arrived in the mornings.

What had happened to his good mood?

"Sorry," he said as he marched past her and headed for his office.

He knew what had happened to his good mood.

Reality had killed it. And here was the further proof. He would have to spend the day dealing with the temporary and completely incompetent PA sent up by Human Resources—and, *merda*, there she was, springing to her feet.

"Good morn—"

"Good morning," Marco snarled. "And sit down,

dammit."

"Sorry, sir. I only—"

*Cristo,* was her voice shaking?

"Yes. I understand." Marco smiled. At least, he hoped he was smiling. "Sorry. I didn't mean to..." She was looking at him as if he'd lost his mind. "Any messages?" he said briskly.

"Yes, sir. I put them on your desk."

Marco thanked her, entered his office, shrugged off his suit jacket, hung it away and went to his desk.

The stack of messages looked three feet high. His regular PA would have winnowed it by more than half. And the very first message was not a good one. The garage needed more insurance information. His PA should have handled it.

Correction.

*Would* have handled it, if she were still here.

Marco reached for the phone, stabbed the button for his HR manager.

"What is happening about finding me an assistant?"

She told him that she had contacted an agency that specialized in administrative assistants of the highest caliber.

"I explained the urgency of the situation, Mr. Santini, and they're sending what they assure me are three excellent candidates for interviews this morning. I'll narrow it to the one who seems most suitable and send her to you for your approval."

One problem down.

Another thousand to go, including one that was personal.

He took a piece of letterhead engraved with his name, gave what he would write a minute's thought before coming up with words that were brief, to the point and not open to interpretation.

*For shared memories.*

He scrawled his name beneath the words, put the

note in an envelope and sealed it, and then he phoned Cartier, just a couple of blocks away on Fifth Avenue, arranged for a duplicate of the diamond bracelet raffled off the night before to be delivered to Jessalyn along with the note, which he sent to the store by messenger.

Excellent.

Now he could concentrate on organizing the data he'd need for his trip to Paris tomorrow morning.

Had Emily ever seen Paris?

Marco frowned.

What a foolish thought. And what was she doing, back in his head?

Maybe he should send something to her, now that he'd sent something to Jessalyn. Not jewelry, of course. Nothing that intimate. Chocolates. Flowers. And a note saying he hoped things would go well for her and if they didn't, she should feel free to get in touch with him and…

And what?

Chocolates and flowers and notes of any kind would be a bad idea. Hadn't he just been telling himself he'd been mistaken in thinking he'd been attracted to her? Yes, she was different from the women he knew and that made her interesting, but the truth was, how long would such an interest last?

He already knew that she was unsophisticated. Her accent told him that she was a girl from somewhere in the South, probably a small town where life moved at a slower pace. He figured she was in her twenties. It was easy to imagine her finishing high school, trying to find work as a pianist—a piano player, he thought, smiling—and, after coming up empty, taking a job in an insurance office or maybe at a small retail shop for a couple of years while she saved up enough money to come north to the Big Apple.

She would know nothing of the life he led. She'd be as uncomfortable as the proverbial fish out of water.

Last night had been a page torn out of time.

Besides, suppose he did send her flowers. Or asked her to dinner. Once she realized who he was, what he was, a man building an empire, no matter how unsophisticated she was, that would change things. Like the easy way she'd dealt with him. Of course it would.

Plus, what would they talk about? Not that his conversations with the women he dated were ever deep and meaningful. Hell, he wasn't looking for deep and meaningful, only that the women who passed through his life fit into it.

Seamlessly.

But he'd bet anything in the world that his rain-soaked tigress would fit into his arms.

Into his bed.

Emily, her skin silken and hot under the stroke of his hands, her mouth sweet and parted to the thrust of his tongue, her body arching against his, her cries of need and desire rising into the silence of the night…

His elbow jerked.

Half the stack of messages tumbled to the floor.

Marco muttered a curse, retrieved them, dumped them on his desk and shot to his feet.

The window wall behind him offered a breathtaking view of the city. He swung toward it, flattened his hands against the cool glass and took long, deep breaths until his mind emptied of everything.

He'd been working too hard lately. He always worked hard but the past few months had been rough. He'd had acquisitions to deal with, the expansion of MS Enterprises into Brazil, endless projects that all required constant attention.

This was the result.

Foolish thoughts. Pointless imaginings. He was, and always had been, a logical man. He didn't waste time daydreaming. He had built his empire on logic. On clear, cool thought.

Perhaps he needed a break.

"Mr. Santini?"

The Paris trip. Then a few days off. He'd fly down to La Tortuga, the island he'd recently bought in the Caribbean. Hadn't he promised himself he'd find time to do that? There was a house there, adequate to stay in until he planned the one that would replace it. Maybe he could begin doing that while he was there.

"Mr. Santini. Sir."

The sun, the sea, the isolation of the white sand beaches and lushly wild interior were the reasons he'd bought the island. Surely, a couple of days in that kind of privacy would restore his equilibrium—

"Mr. Santini. I'm sorry to bother you, sir, but a problem's developed."

Marco frowned and turned to the door. His people knew better than to walk in without knocking. If an efficient PA were at the desk she'd have—

Joe Stein, the head of the design team that had handled the Twenty-two Pascal project, stood in the doorway. Joe had been busy all week with final preparation for the building's grand opening on Wednesday.

Normally, he had a ready smile and bright pink cheeks.

This morning, his face was pale. In fact, he looked as if he were going to be sick.

Marco felt a knot forming in the pit of his belly.

"What problem?"

"You, uh, you remember the plans for the atrium at the Pascal building?"

Marco's frown deepened. Did he remember them? The atrium was the focal point of the restoration. His company had taken what was basically a useless empty space and turned it into a glass box, open to the sun, protected from rain and snow by a sliding glass roof.

"*Si*," he said carefully. "I remember it quite well."

"Yes. Well—well, we've run into some difficulties

with it."

"Dammit, man, don't pussyfoot. What difficulties?"

"The orchids. For the display."

The orchids. White orchids. Ten thousand branching stems of them.

The knot in Marco's gut tightened. "What about them?"

"We're—we're not getting them."

"What do you mean, we're not getting them? I authorized the order months ago. "

"Yes, sir. But—but…"

Stein launched into an explanation that started with a series of tornadoes destroying dozens of greenhouses and ended with a freak hailstorm trapping a huge cargo plane on a runway.

Midway through, Marco held up his hand.

"Get to the point," he snapped. "How many orchids are we getting?"

"None."

Marco could feel his mouth drop open. "None?"

"That's right. None."

"Let me be sure I understand this. Today is Monday. The official opening of Twenty-two Pascal is two days away. The mayor will be there. So will NBC, ABC, FOX and CBS. Vanity Fair is sending a photographer."

"Yes, sir. I know. But—"

"But," Marco said in a low voice that drained the final bit of color from Stein's face, "all anyone will see is an eighteen-foot-square glass room filled with rows of glass risers topped by white ceramic vases filled with… nothing.

Stein's Adam's apple made a noticeable up-and-down track above his dark blue tie.

"I could probably find other flowers."

"But not orchids."

"No. White flowers."

"What kind of white flowers?"

Stein's Adam's apple moved again.

"Well, if I ordered from several dealers, I could mix them. You know. Roses. Tulips. Carnations. Carnations are easy to come by."

"You'll be suggesting daisies next," Marco said coldly, rubbing the nape of his neck as he paced the length of his office. "Dammit," he said, swinging toward the hapless designer, "the whole idea was to provide drama. Visual and aesthetic impact. Elegance."

Stein nodded. "I know."

"There must be some other way to do it."

"How about—how about installing a pond? Maybe a waterfall. Some fish…"

Marco's glower silenced him.

"Birds," Stein said after a couple of seconds. "White bamboo cages full of—what are those big white birds? Cockatoos."

"This is a building, not a zoo! Come up with another idea. What about something you've done before in—where was it you worked? Chicago?"

"Yes. Chicago." Stein's face lit. "I did a terrific display in a big department store."

"What was it?"

"Well, it was seasonal. It was, uh, it was Christmas."

"This is September," Marco said coldly.

"Halloween is coming. Thanksgiving—"

"Pumpkins and turkeys? Get hold of yourself, man! This is not a shopping mall: it is a historic building saved from being razed. I told you what I wanted almost six months ago: a construct that would push back the noise and smells of the streets. Offer tranquility in the midst of a city. An urban oasis."

"I understood the concept, sir. It was why I suggested the orchids. I'd created something similar in the foyer of a concert hall in Chicago. The papers dubbed it an urban island."

"What was it?"

"Well, it wouldn't apply here. I'm not even suggesting that it would—"

"What was it?" Marco said sharply.

"I used candles. All sizes, all shapes—all of them electric," he added quickly, when Marco raised his eyebrows. "There was no danger of fire. And in the center, a Steinway grand."

"A what?"

"A piano. One of those big things you see at concerts. The pianist wore a tux. The real deal, you know, a black tux, the coat with that funny-looking split tail—"

"A white grand piano," Marco said slowly.

"No, sir. It was black—"

"A white piano. The white vases on the glass risers, the vases filled with tall glass candles and alternating with tall white—"

"Lilies," Stein said excitedly. "White candles. White lilies. White piano. A guy in a white tuxedo."

"A woman," Marco said, "in a white evening gown."

Stein nodded his head furiously. "Yes, sir! That would work. We already have the vases. I can get the candles, no sweat. And flowers—we won't need anywhere near as many since we're also using candles. As for the piano—no problem, I'm certain."

"In which case, all we lack is the piano player."

"They call them pianists, sir."

"They call them piano players," Marco said, fighting back the little rush of anticipatory excitement that went through him.

****

Stein left to deal with the piano, the flowers and the candles.

"I'll handle the rest," Marco told him.

"The rest," of course, was Emily.

He'd come away last night without her phone

number, even without her last name but then, he'd never anticipated seeing her again. Getting in touch with her now was only logical. Nothing about it was personal. He needed a piano player. She needed a job. Now that he thought about it, he hadn't really bought into her breezy *Oh, my agent will find me something else.* If it were that easy, she wouldn't have been working in the kind of dive she'd described.

This was business, plain and simple.

He considered going to see her but decided against it. Too personal. A would-be employer would not turn up at a would-be employee's door. Not that he would actually be her employer. This was a temporary job…

"Hell," he muttered, and reached for the phone.

His attorney listened, asked for Emily's address, said he knew just who to contact and would get back to him with the information within the hour.

"Unless you want a full background check."

"I want an address and a phone number," Marco said brusquely. "Nothing more."

Twenty minutes later, he had her last name—Madison—her cell number and her landline number.

All he had to do now was contact her.

Why was he hesitating? What he was about to do was logical. Eminently logical.

Nothing about this was personal.

She needed a job. He needed a piano player. It was a win-win situation, a problem solved for him, a problem solved for her. It might even be more than that for her. This was only a one-day event but it would provide her with excellent media coverage.

That kind of exposure was surely good for an entertainer. Not that he'd gotten the impression she saw herself as an entertainer. He hadn't even gotten the sense that she saw piano as a career. It hadn't been in anything she'd said but in her attitude. Maybe she was still looking for a career.

Whatever. That didn't matter.

Her future was not his concern. Solving Wednesday's problem was.

Still, calling Emily himself struck him as almost as unwise as going to see her.

Marco frowned.

Normally, he'd have told his PA to handle things, but…

But he did have an HR manager.

He dialed her extension, quickly explained that there'd been a change of plans for the Wednesday opening of Twenty-two Pascal.

"Of what, sir?"

Hell, he was an idiot! What would Human Resources know about it?

Marco filled her in on the situation and on how the company was dealing with it.

"Well," the head of HR said cautiously, "that's great news—but what does it have to do with Human Resources?"

Marco cleared his throat.

"Obviously, we need someone to play the piano."

"Ah. Well, sir, unfortunately, I'm afraid I wouldn't know how to go about locating a pianist—"

"A piano player," Marco said, "and I already know of someone. I'll give you her name and number. Call her, explain that we have a one-day job for her and ask her to come in this morning."

"You want me to call this person, sir?"

"Of course," Marco said briskly. "We will be employing her, will we not?"

"Well, yes, but—"

"All hiring at MS Enterprises is done through your office, Mrs. Barnett."

"I really don't know what to ask her, Mr. Santini. I mean, what should I look for in her résumé?"

"Never mind a résumé," Marco said briskly. "Just

call her, tell her what we want and have her come in to sign the necessary documents."

"And if she asks how we know about her, sir?"

Marco put his hand to his forehead. It was an excellent question.

"Never mind."

"But you said—"

"I'll handle this myself."

Was he insane? He was making more of this than necessary. Emily played piano. She needed work. He had a piano. Well, a building his company had restored had a piano or it would have a piano and *Dio,* all he had to do was phone her and tell her he was offering her a job. Easy, especially since he wouldn't even be in town on Wednesday.

He'd be in Paris.

Marco took a deep breath. Picked up the phone. And stared at it.

His mouth was dry.

This was ridiculous! He was behaving like a teenage kid calling a girl for a date. Not that he'd ever been a teenage kid calling a girl for a date. He'd discovered sex at seventeen with the mistress of the rich American who'd hired him to clear out the tangle of trees and shrubs behind the house the man had put up on the cliffs outside Catania.

She'd kept him happy that entire summer, and by the end of it he'd saved enough money to emigrate to the States where he'd worked his ass off doing what he still thought of as donkey labor. Anywhere he could find it.

The girls, long-legged American beauties, had found him.

He punched in the cell number the attorney had given him. It rang and rang and then a robotic voice announced that the number was no longer working.

OK.

Maybe that was a sign…

Except that she had a regular phone as well as the mobile and he had that number, too.

Quickly, he punched in the numbers for the landline. The phone rang five times. Then another electronic voice announced that there was no one there to take the call.

*At the sound of the tone, please leave a message.*

Marco cleared his throat. "Emily. This is Marco Santini. Do you remember me?"

He winced. Of course she would remember him. Not even twelve hours had gone by since they'd met. Since he'd kissed her like a man who'd lost control of his sanity.

"What I mean to say is that I have a job for you. A one-day job. Playing piano." *Stupido! What else would it be?* "At the ceremonial opening of that building we talked about, Twenty-two Pascal. You'll get some good publicity out of it. Press, TV, that kind of thing. We'd intended to fill the atrium with flowers but that fell through and we thought, my designer thought, candles and some flowers and a piano, a white Steinway grand…"

Marco clamped his lips together. Talk about information overload!

"If you are interested, please call my Human Resources manager, Jane Barnett, at 212-555-1740 She is the person who will handle the arrangements. You will meet with her. You will not see me at all…"

He rolled his eyes as he let his pathetic little speech trail off. Then he said a brisk *"Ciao"* and ended the artless call.

****

Wasn't this supposed to be the age of the paperless office?

It wasn't, and without his PA to sift through reports and memos and cull the ones that didn't require his attention, he never got around to compiling the documents he needed for tomorrow's trip to Europe.

Just before noon, he made an attempt at involving the girl sitting in for his former PA. Bad move. Within minutes, she was in tears. When he asked—calmly, he was certain—what the problem was, she said that he talked too fast, wanted her to do too many things at once, and what on earth did he mean when he said "Tell Moscow that I agree." Tell whom in Moscow? And to what did he agree?

Marco started to explain, heard his voice rising, wondered, albeit briefly, if any of this could even remotely be the reason so many assistants flew the coop abandoned that as nonsense and shooed the girl from his office.

He had lunch at his desk—the temp grew so flustered at the idea of phoning in his order that he did it himself. A green salad with oil and that special vinegar on the side. No, he did not know the name but how many types could there be? Cheese on a roll. Not just any cheese. The one his PA's, all of them, always knew to order. And not just any roll. The long one without seeds and, *Cristo,* why would he know what it was called?

The deli clerk who took his call was new—was this a day of new-to-the-job fools? So it was no great surprise that when his lunch arrived, it was the wrong roll, the wrong cheese, and the salad on the side was all wrong.

He stuffed everything back into the bag it had come in and tossed it into the wastebasket.

Coffee. At least he could have coffee. His PA always made it and no way would he ask the trembling girl outside his door to do so.

Marco pushed back his chair and got to his feet. Surely they made coffee in the staff room. The sight of him would probably send everybody scuttling but his mood was going from bad to worse and, frankly, he didn't give a damn whether they scuttled or not.

His phone rang. He grabbed for it and snarled, "What?"

It was the garage, with the first good news of the day. His Ferrari had not been stolen. It had been misplaced.

"Misplaced?"

Misplaced. The manager launched into an explanation. Marco cut him short, thanked him, hung up the phone and made a note to find a different garage.

The phone rang again. "It's Jane Barnett," his HR manager said.

"Mrs. Barnett. Jane. I meant to call."

"Actually, I've been trying to reach your PA."

Marco shuddered. "Yes. So have I. She seems to have disappeared. What of those candidates you were going to interview? How has that worked out? Please tell me you've found one who is suitable."

"Uh," Jane said carefully, "well, I may have found one who is just about perfect."

The second good news of the day. Marco beamed happily as he sank into his chair.

"Do you mean it?"

"She speaks four languages. She's traveled. She's bright. I'm sure she can write up reports. Fairly complex ones, I suspect. As I said, she's just about perfect."

Marco wanted to pump his fist in the air but not yet, not yet.

"Did you explain that she'll have to be prepared to leave the country tomorrow?"

A pause. Then, "Uh, not exactly."

"Because?"

"Because this isn't precisely the job she came here to fill."

"Didn't the agency explain the situation to her?"

"Uh…"

"What are you telling me, Jane? Is she not interested in the position? Did you explain how well it pays?

Seventy-five thousand a year? Health insurance? Vacations? Pension?”

“Uh, I thought you might want to talk with her yourself, Mr. Santini. See, this is a bit confusing. She was here to interview for one thing and I ended up offering her another.”

Marco shut his eyes. Good news, but with an edge.

“Wonderful. I have been dealing with incompetence all morning and now we add the incompetence of a headhunting agency that sends a person to the wrong job. But if this woman is suitable…”

“I believe she is, sir.”

“And what about Ms. Madison? Has she called?”

“Uh…”

*Dio,* another “uh”?

“Never mind. One thing at a time. Send this paragon of efficiency to my office *rapidamente.*”

“That’s why I’m calling, sir. I tried to reach your PA—”

“My temp,” Marco growled. “God forbid she might ever be anyone’s PA.”

“Yes, sir. Right. The point is, she didn’t answer. So I called Executive Reception to tell her that, uh, the candidate is on her way.”

“And?”

“And, uh, before you meet with her I wanted to explain that, uh—”

“Jane,” Marco said through his teeth, “if there is something to explain, explain it.”

“I’m trying to, Mr. Santini, but it’s a little complicated and, uh—”

It was the final “uh” that broke the camel’s back—that, and the  tap on his door that told him his terrified and definitely temporary assistant was about to step into his office.

Marco swung toward the door as it opened, his patience, what little remained of it, shot to hell.

"What in the name of God do you want now?" he roared at his PA. Except it wasn't his PA.

It was the woman who had kept him awake most of the night, the woman he'd hoped he'd never see again.

Emily Madison.

# CHAPTER FIVE

Emily's day had got off to a truly hideous start.

Well, why wouldn't it? Her night had certainly been a mess.

She still couldn't believe what she'd done. Losing her temper, losing her job…

Nola wasn't home. She had a boyfriend, an actor, and she often stayed at his place. That was fine with Emily but last night; she'd have given anything to have Nola there so she'd have had someone to talk to. She'd have told her about the disaster at the Tune-In. And she'd have broken the news that she wasn't going to come up with her half of this month's rent.

The sooner she got that over with, the better.

And then there was what had happened with that man. Marco Santini.

That kiss.

Exhausted as she was, Emily still hadn't been able to fall asleep. She'd gotten up, made a cup of tea, paced the tiny apartment, turned the TV on, stared at it blankly and then paced some more.

At five, she'd crawled into bed, dragged the blanket over her head and decided she just wasn't going to think about any of it. If she just got an hour's sleep…

Which was why she'd pretended not to hear Nola come in and climb into her bed on the other side of the curtain they'd hung between the two beds in the pathetic pretense that they each had more than four feet of privacy.

Within minutes, she'd heard Nola's breathing turn slow and even.

If only hers would do the same, but then, she had weighty things on her mind. No money. No job.

Marco Santini.

And wasn't that ridiculous?

He had kissed her. So what? She wasn't a child. She'd been kissed before.

But not like that.

Or maybe the truth was that no kiss had ever affected her that way. She liked kissing. Liked sex. Even though she'd always thought it was a little overrated.

Lissa and Jaimie sometimes teased her about her attitude.

Or her lack of one.

Always gently, of course, because they were her best friends, but she had never been the one to come home after a date flushed from what had gone on in the back seat of somebody's Chevy.

On the other hand, she had never been the one to sob from the pain of a broken heart.

"Why would any woman in her right mind get involved with a man?" Jaimie had demanded in a tight voice during a three-way Skype session a couple of weeks ago.

"A damned good question," Lissa had said.

Emily had looked at her computer monitor, from one sister's face to the other's.

"Uh, you guys want to talk about it?' she'd finally asked.

The answers had been *no* and *no*, and when the call ended, Emily had shaken her head the same way she had in the past and wondered how her bright, beautiful, talented sisters could be such fools when it came to men.

Right.

And now, after—what?—one kiss from a stranger, she was suddenly an expert on what men and sex were all about?

"Ridiculous," she muttered. And flinched. Because *ridiculous* wasn't even close to describing what had happened last night.

She had humiliated herself.

He'd kissed her. OK. People kissed all the time. She could have stood still and let it happen. She could have turned her face away. She could have said, with Victorian indignation, that driving her home did not entitle him to take liberties.

Instead, she'd—she'd wrapped herself around him like an octopus. He'd had to peel her off. Then he'd mumbled something polite and escaped as fast as was humanly possible.

Humiliating didn't come close to describing it.

Emily groaned and burrowed deeper under the blankets.

"Stop it," she whispered. "Just—just put it out of your mind. You'll never see him again so why keep thinking about what an absolute fool you made of yourself?"

What she needed was sleep. A couple of hours, anyway. The day looming before her was going to be tough enough to handle without adding in a brain drained by exhaustion. She'd have to face Nola. Call Max Pergozin and if he had nothing for her, start the horrible thing known as searching for employment. And as what? Who would employ her? The city was filled with women like her, their heads packed with useless academic nonsense.

Emily yawned. Yawned again. And drifted, mercifully, into sleep. And, unmercifully, into a dream about a tall, gorgeous hunk of masculinity, with dark hair, dark eyes and a sexy accent, who kissed her and then didn't stop at kissing her.

She was moaning when the piercing ring of the telephone jolted her awake.

Let voice mail take the call. She'd just lie here, close her eyes, see if she could recapture the dream.

*At the sound of the tone, please leave a message.*

"PICK UP THIS PHONE, MADISON! YOU HEAR ME? PICK UP THE GODDAMNED PHONE!"

Emily shoved the covers aside, flew to the wall of ancient, Lilliputian-sized appliances that passed for a kitchen and grabbed the receiver.

"Mr. Pergozin?"

"YOU ARE FIRED, GIRLY. FIRED! YOU GOT THAT?"

Emily winced, propped the phone against her shoulder, opened the cupboard and searched for a bottle of aspirin.

"Mr. Pergozin. I know you're annoyed but—"

"ANNOYED? ANNOYED?"

"Please. If you could just lower your voice—"

"Fine. I'll lower my voice. Is this low enough? YOU WILL NEVER WORK IN THIS TOWN AGAIN!"

Emily wrenched open the aspirin bottle, dumped three tablets on the counter, turned on the water in the sink, popped the tablets into her mouth, bent down, angled her head, slurped at the water and swallowed hard. The tablets stuck in her throat and she coughed, dragged in a breath and said, "Look, I don't know what Gus told you but—"

"He told me what I already suspected. That you're a dainty prima donna with no more brains than a cockroach!"

"If you'd just listen—"

"Didn't you hear me? You are fired!"

Emily stood straighter.

"You can't fire me. I'm your client. I'm the one who does the firing."

"Do I give a crap how you say it? You are done. Got that? D-O-N-E. Done!"

Emily could feel her mouth trembling. "This isn't fair! Whatever Gus said—"

"I just told you what he said. Want me to tell you again?"

"Gus owes me money for—"

Max laughed.

"He owes me! I worked four nights and—"

"Fine. Sue him."

"Mr. Pergozin. Please. There were extenuating circumstances—"

"That's it. Use big words. Try and impress me with that fancy degree. You don't got the brains you were born with; blowing a job my other clients would have killed for."

Really? she thought, but she forced herself not to say that. Instead, she bit the bullet and said that what had happened was unfortunate, and that she would take any other gig he had…

Max laughed and laughed and laughed.

"I take it that's a no," Emily said with all the poise she could muster, and then she slammed the phone back into its cradle. "Stupid, horrid, miserable, awful little man!"

"Problem?" Nola said carefully.

Emily swung toward her. Her roommate held out a mug of coffee. She grabbed it and took a long swallow.

"That was my agent."

"Uh-huh."

"He, ah, he's not happy."

"No kidding."

Emily sighed. "I lost my job at the Tune-In."

"Oh, sweetie! That's too bad."

"Yeah," Emily said unhappily. "And Max said—"

"Never mind Max. How are you for cash?"

Emily felt her face heat. "Not good. In fact, I hate to ask but—"

"Not to worry. I'll take care of this month's rent."

"Oh, that's lovely! Thank you. As soon as I find something else, I'll—"

"Actually—actually, there's something I have to tell you, too."

Nola was biting her fingernails. After a while, you knew how to read a roommate. Nola's biting her fingernails was not a good sign.

"What?"

"That part I auditioned for last week? The second lead in the touring company production of *Coming up Roses*, remember? Well, I got it!"

"Oh, wow! I'm so happy for—"

"Yeah. But the thing is, we head out next week. And we'll be gone for six months. So—so—"

The floor seemed to tilt under Emily's feet.

"You're moving out?"

"See, they offered the role to somebody else and she said *yes* but then something went wrong and she had to back out and that's why they only just contacted me and—"

"That's fine. No, really, I mean it. That's why Max called. He, ah, he's got something even better lined up."

"You sure? 'Cause it didn't sound as if—"

"Oh he's all bluster. He's going to call me back with the details."

By the time the phone rang again, Nola had left for the theater. Emily was in the shower. Her pulse soared. Maybe it really *was* Max.

By the time she skidded to a stop in the tiny kitchen, the call had gone to voice mail.

"Emily?" a husky voice said. "Pick up if you're there. It's Marco. Marco Santini."

Her heart thudded.

She hadn't expected him to call. Why would she? She'd made a fool of herself, and if she'd had any doubt about that, all she had to do was remind herself that he hadn't even asked for her number. He hadn't mentioned seeing her again. If anything, his last words had struck her as not just "goodbye" but "goodbye and it's been nice knowing you."

Her face heated at the memory.

So, why was he calling? How was he calling? He didn't have her number.

She reached for the phone. Changed her mind. Stared at it. Waited for him to speak. Finally, he did.

He spoke briskly. Impersonally. He was offering her a job playing piano at the opening of that building, the one she'd told him she lived in because common sense had told her not to let a stranger know her address.

Too bad common sense hadn't told her not to let him kiss her.

Not that it had meant anything. The proof of that was hearing his crisp assurances that she would have no involvement with him whatsoever. She would not see him or deal with him. She would be interviewed by a Jane Barnett in his company's Human Resources Department.

The message ended.

Emily slumped against the wall.

There had to be a better word than *humiliating*.

What, was she his charity deed for the week? Saving her from the elements. Finding her a job.

"To hell with you, Mr. Santini," she told the telephone. "You can just take your big-deal offer and—and—"

And offer it to somebody else.

She scowled.

Was she nuts? A job was a job. Who gave a damn if it came from him? She wouldn't have to see him, speak to him, have anything to do with him.

Of course she'd take his offer.

She grabbed the phone, replayed his message, scribbled down Jane Barnett's name and telephone number. Two minutes later, she'd arranged for a one-thirty appointment at MS Enterprises on Madison Avenue.

She'd moved quickly after that.

By twelve thirty, she was dressed for corporate America. Thank goodness for the clothes she'd brought from Texas to New York. Cream silk blouse. Gray wool suit. High-heeled black pumps. A pair of small gold hoop earrings.

She looked in the mirror. Good. Fine. Demure but stylish.

She was ready.

She took the N train to Fifth Avenue and 53rd Street, walked to Madison Avenue, checked the numbers of the buildings…

Her jaw dropped.

She'd figured out that Marco Santini was rich and powerful but this was more than she'd imagined. MS Enterprises was not housed in a touch-the-clouds skyscraper—it *was* the skyscraper.

This job, a one-day gig for a corporation like this, could be a lot more important than all those miserable weeks at the Tune-In.

Back straight, shoulders squared, she went briskly through the doors and to the lobby reception desk. She identified herself, one of the receptionists made a call, smiled pleasantly and directed her to the tenth floor.

At Human Resources, another smiling individual handed her a stack of papers and a pencil. She spent ten minutes filling out the usual stuff required for corporate job interviews, not just her name and address but, basically, her life story: schooling, degrees, skills, etc. It seemed a waste of time, considering they were going to hire her for one day and only to play the piano but she'd gone this route before, even when she'd applied for a waitressing job at a fancy Upper East Side restaurant.

At precisely one thirty, she was ushered into Jane Barnett's office.

"Ms. Madison," the HR manager said pleasantly, "I must be honest and tell you that I don't know very much about music and musicians."

Emily smiled just as pleasantly.

"Then I must be equally honest and tell you that I don't know much about MS Enterprises."

Polite laughter on both sides. Then Jane Barnett motioned her to a chair opposite her desk and began reading Emily's application.

Emily waited, feet placed neatly together, hands folded in her lap. She'd been through this before, often enough to know that the reading would take perhaps two minutes.

Wrong.

Barnett started by skimming the document. Midway through, she stopped, looked at Emily and then went back and started at the beginning. She read more and more slowly, looked up, stared at Emily, looked down, looked up…

Emily gave a discreet cough. "Is there a problem?"

Barnett put down the application, removed her glasses, then put them on again.

"Impressive," she said. "Four languages?"

"Well, yes. But—"

"A degree in art. Dean's list. Graduated with honors."

"Did I give too much information? I only meant to answer the quest—"

"I'll bet you loved academia," Barnett said, leaning forward. "You know, doing research, writing papers, taking notes, that sort of thing."

What, Emily thought, did any of this have to do with her skills as a piano player? Unless… Her mouth went dry. Was this leading to a request for references? Max wouldn't give any. Gus wouldn't, either. In fact, he'd probably do his best to —

"Am I correct, Ms. Madison?"

"Yes. I mean, I was a good student but—but I love playing piano. I took lessons for—"

"Oh, of course. I'm sure you're a fine pianist. But you have such an, uh, an interesting résumé… Have you been to Europe? South America?" Barnett picked up a pencil, tapped it on the desk. "I don't suppose you spent any time abroad…?"

"Actually, my father was—is—um, he's in the military, so—"

"Very interesting."

"Right." Emily hesitated. "But, you know, about the piano thing. This Wednesday, right? I don't know much about it. For instance, how many hours will it involve? What's the starting time? Would you want me to play popular music? Contemporary? Classical? Light?"

"Oh. That."

That? *That?*

"We can work out those details later, Emily. May I call you Emily?"

"Sure. But—"

"For now, let's move right along to the interview."

Baffled, Emily stared at her. "I thought this was the interview."

"Yes, of course, but…"

"Oh. I understand. You want me to audition."

Barnett smiled brightly. "Exactly. If you'd take the elevator to the fiftieth floor—the executive offices. I'll phone ahead and tell them you're coming. And, Emily?" She rose and stuck out her hand. "Good luck."

What a strange woman, Emily thought as she took the elevator to the top floor. And what an odd place to house a piano, but then, what did she really know about corporate procedure?

The car doors opened onto a vast, high-ceilinged space filled with light. Double glass doors led to an attractive receptionist, seated at her desk with a telephone at her ear.

"You must be Emily."

"Yes, that's right."

The receptionist smiled. "HR called to say you were on your way. In fact, I'm trying to reach the boss's PA and announce you, but she's not picking up. Well, never mind. Mrs. Barnett said to move you right along.

Through those doors, please, turn left and go to the end of the corridor."

Impressive, Emily thought as she followed directions. The doors were massive-looking but opened at the touch of her hand; the corridor was hung with brilliantly colored works of modern art, and the carpet underfoot was so deep that her heels threatened to sink into it and disappear.

Eventually, the corridor opened onto another huge, brightly lit space. A waiting room, obviously: teak-and-leather chairs, a pair of couches, a big coffee table and, just far enough away to command some privacy, a desk, a chair and a cluster of office machines—printer, fax—arranged outside a set of teak double doors.

The desk was unattended. And after the handsome, sleek furniture, the artwork, the reception area, it was, well, out of place.

Papers were strewn across the surface and piled in teetering stacks. A computer monitor blinked in woeful silence. Two drawers were half opened. A mug of murky black liquid stood next to a space-age telephone, lights blinking in desperation.

For the first time, Emily felt uneasy. She took an inadvertent step back.

What was this? The Mad Hatter's tea party? That peculiar interview and now this unlikely mess, topped off by the closed teak doors…

It wasn't too late.

She'd considered her options.

Wait until somebody showed up.

Or retrace her steps straight down to the lobby…

And straight out of a chance at a job. A paycheck. Maybe even the prospect of meeting someone in the art world.

Really, she had decided, there wasn't a choice.

So she'd squared her shoulders. Breathed deep. Marched past the disaster area of a desk directly to the closed double doors, knocked more politely than she'd figured the situation warranted, opened the doors…

And been treated to a snarled "What?" and a man she'd never wanted to see again, Marco Santini, all six feet three inches of gorgeous male, with a look on his face that made it absolutely clear he felt the exact same way.

# CHAPTER SIX

Emily stared at the apparition that was Marco Santini. He stared back. Then he took a step forward.

"Emily?"

"Mr. Santini?"

"It's Marco. And what—"

And what are you doing here? he'd almost said, but from the look on her face he suspected she was about to ask him the same question.

"I don't—I didn't—" Her gaze swept past him, raked his entire office before returning to him. "Where's the piano?"

"The what?"

"The piano."

Marco shook his head. "What piano?"

"The one I'm here to play."

"Wednesday," he said, "you're playing on—"

"Oh, I know that. But I assume Mrs. Barrett—"

"Mrs. Barnett," he said, as if it mattered. "It's Jane Barnett."

Emily nodded. "She sent me up here. I figured it was to audition." The tip of her tongue appeared and slicked lightly over her bottom lip. "But not for you. Your message said you wouldn't—that I wouldn't be seeing you."

"No. I mean, yes. I mean…" Marco walked to his desk, put down the papers he'd been holding and ran both hands through his hair. "Obviously, there's been some kind of mix-up."

"Yes. Probably my fault." She turned toward the door. "It's been nice seeing—"

"Don't go."

He spoke the words in a rush. She looked at him and he cleared his throat.

"I mean, now that you're here… How are you?" He bit back a groan. Was he a brilliant conversationalist or what? "What I mean is, I wondered if you were OK, if you'd caught a chill last night."

"Oh. No. No, I'm fine, thank you." She hesitated. "What about you? You must have been as soaked as I was."

"I'm fine."

"You didn't even have the protection of your jacket." Her eyes widened. "Your jacket! I should have brought it with me. I wasn't thinking. To your office. Your office building I mean, I certainly didn't expect to see you…" Emily clamped her lips together. "Sorry," she said, after a couple of seconds. "I'm just a little surprised. I didn't think you'd be auditioning me."

X-rated images shot through his head. He swung away, busied himself straightening the papers he'd dumped on his desk.

"No need for that," he said briskly. "I already know that you can do the job."

She gave a little laugh. "But you don't. Not really. I mean, you only have my word for it."

She was right.

He'd arranged to hire her without knowing anything about her except what she'd told him. That wasn't how he did business. Before he signed a contract, bought a property, hired anyone who would be part of his staff, he did as much research as possible.

And yet he'd hired this woman to help launch a boutique project that had consumed his time and energy for months when for all he knew, the only thing she could play was "Chopsticks."

Or "New York, New York." Remembering what she'd said, he gave a soft laugh.

"What?"

"I was thinking about Wednesday. Just play "New York, New York" if somebody asks. You do that, everything will be fine."

They both laughed. The palpable tension in the room eased, if only a little. Then Emily touched the tip of her tongue to the middle of her bottom lip again.

It was disconcerting.

So was the fact that his waif of the storm was gone.

No bare feet. No rain-soaked silk dress clinging to her like a second skin. No soft curls begging for his touch.

She was the epitome of professional competence. Wool suit. Silk blouse. Black pumps. Hair tamed into submission and drawn back in a no-nonsense, nape-of-the-neck ponytail.

He felt a pang of regret.

The formal Emily was as beautiful as he'd remembered but there'd been something charming about the less formal one.

And wasn't that a ridiculous thought? Who cared about that? All that mattered was that she could pull off the performance on Wednesday…

Dammit!

"You'll need a white formal gown." Her eyebrows rose. "For Wednesday," he said. "I don't know how specific I was when I left that message, but the overall theme will be dramatic. Romantic. White candles, white flowers, white piano… And you in something long and white."

"I don't have—"

"Not a problem. Find something and send me the bill."

"I beg your pardon?"

"I'll pay for it. The company will pay for it the same as for the flowers, the piano… Everything." He waited for her to say something. Anything. What he didn't want her to say was goodbye. "Well," he said briskly. "This was a very nice surprise."

"I'm sorry to have bothered you. The message you

left was very clear. I don't know how things got so confused—"

"Jane. Jane Barnett. She must have misunderstood."

"Whatever, my apologies. As for your jacket—"

"Forget the jacket."

"Don't be silly! I'll have it cleaned and pressed and delivered to—"

"Emily. About that message…"

He hesitated. The lie would be so simple. Something about being busy, about being rushed for time…

But he couldn't lie to her. He didn't want to.

"The message," he said in a low voice, "was stupid and self-serving."

He had caught her by surprise. He could see it in the way her eyes widened, in the way her lips parted.

His belly knotted.

He wanted to take her in his arms and kiss those gently parted lips as he had kissed them last night, wanted her to respond to him as she had last night.

"The truth is that I ached to see you again."

Emily knew what she was supposed to say. Not the exact words, maybe, but the sense of them. A woman played cool when a man who interested her admitted he was interested, too. That was the time to flirt a little. Bat your lashes. Smile up into his eyes.

"I didn't want to leave you last night."

His voice was low. His words were sexy. She told herself not to answer…

"Then why did you?" she said, and held her breath.

"I am not the kind of man a girl like you should be involved with, *cara*."

Emily stared up into eyes that had gone from midnight blue to obsidian. He was arrogant. Incredibly arrogant. She would have been able to laugh at his egocentricity, but this was different. His certainty that she would have let him stay. His conviction that he was wrong for her.

It was different because he was right. About everything.

She did want him.

And he was probably more than she could handle.

He was a conqueror. A man who knew what he wanted and took it. Power emanated from him. It was in his eyes, the set of his shoulders, the very way he seemed to fill the room.

"Emily."

She looked up at him. Her breathing quickened. His eyes were so dark. Was there a color deeper than obsidian?

"Leave now," he said thickly. "Before—"

She walked to him, curled her fingers into his shirt, rose on her toes and pressed her mouth to his. He didn't move. Didn't touch her. He stood tall and straight and for what seemed the longest moment of her life, she thought she'd made a mistake

Then he groaned, gathered her into his arms and captured her lips with his.

The earth spun.

She clung to him more tightly because if she didn't, surely she would fall.

He whispered her name against her mouth; she whispered his and he cursed softly and swung her up into his arms.

She buried her face against his throat. Wound her arms around his neck. Trembled as he carried her across the room to a long, wide sofa and lowered her to it.

*What are you doing?* a voice inside Marco said.

She was all the things he'd thought. Naïve. Unsophisticated. He could tell by the way she was responding to him. Nothing held back. Nothing of the temptress. She was making little sounds that went straight through him, whimpers of need that a woman with more experience would not so readily make the first time a man took her in his arms to make love to her.

And this was his office.

He didn't bring his personal life into this space. Never.

Never, he thought, and then he stopped thinking, sank to his knees in front of her, drew her forward and kissed her forehead. Her eyes, her mouth. *Dio,* that mouth! He caught her bottom lip between his teeth, bit lightly and she opened to him, offered him her sweet taste.

"Please," she whispered, "Marco, please…"

He groaned, thrust his hands into her hair. The band with which she'd secured the ponytail broke; her hair tumbled loose, fell over his fingers like fine silk. He buried his face in the shining strands and then he took her mouth again, kissed her and kissed her, each time taking the kiss deeper.

Finally, he drew back, framed her face with his hands and said her name. She opened her eyes. They were blurred with desire, the pupils enormous.

He felt the last of his self-control slipping away.

He took her hands. Brought her to her feet. He wanted to undress her. Strip away the layers that separated them. Take her naked into his arms. Feel her skin against his. Inhale her scent. Put his mouth to her, everywhere. Taste her, everywhere. Mark her as his, as his, as his…

The phone rang.

Maybe it had been ringing for a while.

He couldn't tell. He couldn't tell anything except that he wanted the woman in his arms, as he could not remember ever wanting a woman before.

But the phone was persistent.

*Brring. Brring. Brring.*

Emily blinked. She looked at him like a woman awakening from a deep sleep.

"The telephone…"

"It will stop."

He drew her to him. Ran one hand down her spine, Spread it over her bottom. Lifted her into him and she gasped; her head fell back when she felt his erect flesh press against her.

*Brring. Brring. Brring.*

*Merda!*

One last slow, amazing kiss. Then he slid his arm around her waist and drew her with him to the desk and depressed the speaker button.

"Yes," he said, trying not to sound like a man who might kill the person on the other end of the line.

It was Jane Barnett.

Marco took a deep breath. "What is it, Jane? I am—I'm busy."

"Sir. I just wanted to know how things are going."

Marco nuzzled Emily's hair away from her face. Her cheeks were a bright pink; her skin was hot against his lips.

"Things?" he said.

"Uh, yes, sir. I sent someone up to see you. That young woman who came about the piano job…"

"You mean, Ms. Madison."

Emily's eyes shot to his.

"Yes, sir. Is she there?"

"She is. And this is not the best time for this conversation, Jane. Ms. Madison and I are—are talking."

Emily's color deepened.

"Well, that's good, then. You see, I've been trying to reach your PA but—"

"My PA seems to have, ah, abandoned ship, but Ms. Madison and I don't require her services."

Emily pulled away from his arm. He tugged her back to him. She shook her head, put her hand on his chest. Reluctantly, he let go of her.

"Well, I'm relieved to hear it. Would I be correct in assuming you and Ms. Madison have hit it off?"

"Jane," Marco said sharply, "surely this conversation

can wait."

"I'm just so relieved, Mr. Santini. I know you asked me to hire Ms. Madison to play at that opening Wednesday, but she's so perfect for what you really need…"

"Excuse me?"

Emily straightened her jacket. Her skirt. She ran her hands through her hair, tucked it behind her ears and sat down in one of the chairs by his desk.

"I suspect she'll be the best PA you've ever had."

Marco blinked.

"The best what?"

"PA. Personal assistant. Actually, you might want to consider her your administrative assistant." Jane hesitated. "I left that message with your current PA. Didn't she give it to you?"

Marco strode the length of his office. Had he missed something? He must have. What in hell was the woman talking about?

He asked her exactly that.

"You're not making sense," he growled. "Ms. Madison will perform at the opening of Twenty-two Pascal."

"Only if you insist. Sir."

The "sir" had been tacked on. No one with a brain would not have heard it as either a reprimand or a questioning of his sanity or perhaps both, but if anyone was insane here, it was surely not him.

"Meaning what, exactly?"

"Meaning that once I read her employment application, I realized her potential."

"Her potential as what? Ms. Madison plays the piano. Why would I see her in any other capacity?"

"Why, indeed?" Emily said from right behind him.

Marco turned around. Emily had gotten to her feet. She was standing with her chin elevated, her eyes narrowed.

His narrowed, too. What in hell was going on? His waif had turned into a cool-looking businesswoman. The businesswoman had morphed into a temptress. Now, she seemed to have another transformation coming on. The tigress, from the expression on her face.

"It's about you," he said, trying to keep his voice low and his temper under control. He put his hand over the receiver. "You, and the fact that you seem to have approached my HR manager about a job I had not offered you."

"You don't know what you're talking about!"

"Mr. Santini?"

Jane Barnett's voice rang in his ear. Marco uncovered the telephone.

"Yes. I'm here."

"Ms. Madison is eminently qualified, sir."

"I don't know what Ms. Madison told you, Jane, but—"

"I didn't tell her anything," Emily hissed.

"—but whatever it was, she is not a candidate for the position as my administrative assistant."

"May I ask the reason, sir?"

The reason. The reason. Could it have anything to do with the fact that he never mixed business with pleasure? That if Barnett was correct—though, of course, that was impossible but still, if by some strange twist of fate she were—hiring Emily to work for him would mean any other relationship was out of the question.

No.

He would never be so crass. So chauvinistic. So self-centered.

"Sir?

"Ms. Madison's qualifications are limited."

*"Testa di cazzo,"* Emily snarled.

Was he going crazy? Had Emily the Innocent really just called him a dickhead?

Shocked, he swung around just in time to see her

pluck her handbag from the chair where she'd left it and head for the door.

Marco reached out and grabbed her arm.

"Let go!"

His fingers tightened around her elbow.

"Dammit, let go!"

"Jane. I am afraid I'm busy right now—"

"Have you looked at her employment application? I faxed it to your temp."

Emily glared at him. He glared back. She kicked him in the shin. Marco pushed her against the wall, raised a finger to warn her not to move, wrenched open the door, marched to the fax machine and ripped two pages from its belly.

"Sir? I said, have you looked at—"

Marco disconnected. He grabbed Emily's arm and stepped back inside his office,

He held out her employment application.

"Is this yours? Did you fill this out?"

"I did—but then, I had no idea you had already categorized me as—as whatever it is you think I am."

"You're distorting this entire thing. There is nothing wrong with—with—"

"With working in a bar."

"Yes. No. *Dio,* did I say that?"

"You didn't have to." Emily folded her arms. "I get it now. You were on your way home from that charity something or other—"

"A dinner. And what has that to do with anything?"

"You were on your way home from a la-di-da party where the whole idea is to convince everybody that you're richer than they are."

That was precisely what those parties were all about, but he'd sooner have swallowed his tongue than admit how perfect her description was.

"You know nothing of these things," Marco snapped.

She did, of course. She'd endured enough of them, but why tell him that when he was so certain he knew all there was to know about her?

"You were feeling pretty good about yourself. Big car. Fancy mistress."

"Jessalyn is not my mistress!" True enough. She wasn't, not anymore.

"And then, from out of nowhere, you saw me. The twenty-first century version of—of the poor little matchstick girl!"

"What is a matchstick girl? And what in hell are you talking about?"

"A waif," she said, and the way he looked at her told her she'd scored again. "A pathetic creature in desperate need of help from the all-powerful Marco Santini."

"This is ridiculous!"

Emily stepped forward, eyes glittering. She unfolded her arms and jabbed her index finger into the center of his chest.

"And there it was. Another opportunity for you to feel smug."

"Stop jabbing me!"

"Look at this building," she said, jabbing harder. "This office! How many little old ladies did you have to steal from to afford such—such opulence?"

"This is insane!"

It probably was. Her brothers were rich as Midas and she knew damned well they'd never stolen from anybody, but why stop when she was on such a self-satisfying roll?

"That offer of a job. Wow. The ultimate in—in welfare for the matchstick girl."

Marco grabbed her hand, folded it within his own. "*This* is not crazy! *You* are!"

"Let me tell you something, Mr. Santini. I am not whatever you've decided I am." Emily jerked her head toward the two-paged employment application. "Read it."

"I have no interest in—"

"You're supposed to humor crazy people. Well, humor me." She snatched the application from his hand and all but jammed it under his nose." "Read!"

Marco ground his teeth together. He looked at the application.

"Read it out loud!"

"Name: Emily Madison."

"Not that. Education. Start there."

"Education," he said, trying for bored and getting satisfyingly close. "University of Texas at Austin. BA in art history. Minor in…" He looked up. Emily had folded her arms again. The expression on her face would have turned water to ice. "Minor in… philosophy?"

"Go on."

"Dean's list, eight semesters. Phi Beta—Phi Beta Kappa…"

He lifted his gaze to Emily. She was smiling with all her teeth. Years back, picking up a few bucks crewing on a boat off the coast of Long Island, he'd seen less impressive smiles on sharks.

"There's more."

There certainly was. She spoke French, Spanish, Italian and Chinese.

"Chinese?" he heard himself say.

"Unfortunately, only Mandarin."

That brought his head up. No smile this time. The apology had been dead serious.

Another look at the application. Jane had scrawled a note in the margin. He read it aloud: "Ms. Madison has traveled in Europe, South America and Asia."

This time, when he looked at Emily, there was no discernible expression on his face.

"Playing piano in a bar," she said coldly, "does not mean the absence of a functional brain."

"I never thought that!"

"Doing what I almost did a little while ago, on the other hand, does."

"Doing what…?" Marco shook his head. "Making love?"

"We weren't going to make love, we were—we were going to have sex."

"I apologize for my lack of finesse."

He spoke coldly. She couldn't blame him. She'd made an ass of herself, and whose fault, really, was that?

Hers, of course.

The truth was, *she* was the one who was embarrassed about playing at the Tune-In. Dammit, she was embarrassed about her life. The useless major. The even more useless minor. Her absolute failure at anything and everything that might even come close to success.

As for what had happened here…

He was right to apologize. It had been his fault. Not hers. He had seduced her…

*Liar!* She'd been as much a part of it as he had. She, the woman who couldn't understand hookups, who never slept with a man until, as Lissa had once said, she knew him so well that sleeping with him was just another boring event—she had been ready and willing to get on that couch and tear off a stranger's clothes while he tore off hers.

It was a harsh reality check but a necessary one.

Emily forced her gaze to meet Marco's.

"You don't have to apologize for anything," she said stiffly. "I'm an adult. I take full responsibility for my actions. I should never have come here today." Back straight, shoulders locked, she started past him. "Now if you'll excuse me…"

Marco stretched his arm across the open door.

"Not so fast."

They were inches apart. Emily was glaring at him. Despite what she'd just said, he could see that she blamed him for what had happened.

Perhaps she was right.

He was the man. Men were supposed to be in full

control at all times. He lived by that code; it was one of the things that had made him a success in business. He trusted people who worked for him, but the ultimate responsibility for actions that affected him belonged to him.

It was the same way in his relationships with women.

Not that he had "relationships." Not since his divorce. The word was a female concept and loaded with the sort of emotional baggage women demanded and smart men ignored, but the point was, he was accountable for what had happened just now.

For what had almost happened.

His gaze moved over Emily's face. She was flushed; her eyes glittered. Her mouth was faintly swollen; she was breathing just a little too hard.

She looked like a woman who had just slipped from a man's arms, and despite everything, that was where he wanted her.

What would she do if he reached for her? Would she protest and try to pull away—or would she admit that what had happened was not over? That it couldn't be over until she was naked beneath him, her arms around his neck, her legs around his hips, his hard flesh buried deep within her?

*Dio,* this was not a line of thought to pursue!

It was dangerous.

It was also pointless.

If he'd thought she wasn't the kind of woman who would fit into his world before, he was certain of it now.

She was argumentative. He didn't like that in women. A little backbone, a little independence of thought was one thing, but his days were filled with arguments of one kind or another. Why would he want to face more of them at night?

And this thing about sex. She wasn't just unsophisticated, she was foolish. That remark about them having sex as opposed to making love…

He'd used the polite euphemism women preferred, but did she honestly believe sex was ever about the heart? He'd made that mistake once and, dammit, he'd already thought back to that time earlier today and the lesson it had taught him, that sex was about physical desire and the fulfillment of hunger, and that any emotion aside from the one of pleasure was fodder for fools.

The only thing Emily Madison had going for her was that damnable job application.

Employer and employee. That was the one relationship that would work. And he never, not once, had taken such a relationship any further. Work was work. Play was play and, as the old saying went, never the twain should meet.

The truth was, he'd had a couple of very attractive assistants. The one before the last, in fact, had been beautiful. Or had she been the one prior to that? Whatever. He really had not noticed until a CEO he'd met with had commented on her looks.

"You're a clever SOB, Santini," the guy had leered, "having such a good-looking piece of ass on your payroll."

Marco had been affronted on his PA's behalf—and on his own. He'd never noticed she was stunning, never thought of her as a woman…

Never wanted to kiss her or undress her or taste her breasts, and how in hell could he even consider hiring Emily when his head was full of those images?

"Excuse me."

Could he get past that? Could he see her as just another office fixture?

"Mr. Santini. Will you please step—"

"I have a proposition to offer you."

Emily laughed.

"A business proposition."

"My God, are we still on that? Trust me. I'd sooner

go back to that bar than take that job playing for you on Wednesday."

"But you can't go back to that bar," Marco said in a silken voice. "Can you, Ms. Madison?"

"That's my business."

Her chin shot up. The gesture of defiance made the desire to pull her into his arms all the more difficult to ignore… and what he was about to say all the more foolish. No. He was due in Paris tomorrow; this French deal would be one of the most important of his career.

"Mr. Santini. I have asked you, politely, to step aside."

"Is the information on that application accurate?"

"It certainly is."

"Do you have a passport?"

"What is this? Twenty Questions?"

"A passport, Emily. Do you have one?"

"Yes, of course, but—"

"My personal assistants work very hard."

"They have my sympathy."

"In truth, they are—if I am fortunate—more administrative assistants than personal ones."

"Thanks to the sexual discrimination laws."

How he wanted to silence that soft, lovely mouth!

"Very amusing."

"I thought so."

He cleared his throat. Took his hand from the doorjamb. Folded his arms over his chest.

"I am offering you the job. As my PA."

"Now who's being amusing?"

"You must be ready to leave the country immediately."

"You don't hear well, do you? I don't want to play your piano, let alone—"

"We fly to Paris tomorrow."

"Good for you. As for me, I'm out of here. Goodbye, Mr. Santini."

He glared at her. Then he inclined his head and stepped aside. She marched past him and the door slammed shut behind her.

What a dreadful man!

All arrogance. All ego. All I-am-the-center-of-the-universe.

Well, in his world, he probably was.

The confrontation had left her drained. Shaky. It wasn't that kiss. It wasn't the way it had felt when he'd touched her. Kissed her. The way it would have felt if he'd stripped away her clothing, stripped away his, come down on top of her…

She jumped as the door flew open and banged against the wall.

"That next PA of mine," he said, "the one for whom you offer sympathy… Did I mention what her pay will be?"

"An autographed photo? A bowl of gruel?" Emily fluttered her lashes. "A warm kennel?"

"One hundred thousand a year."

She blinked. "Dollars?"

"Plus health coverage. Paid holidays. Four weeks of vacation. And a clothing allowance."

"A clothing allowance?"

He shrugged. "My assistant travels with me. Attends meetings with me. Business lunches, dinners, whatever. It is imperative she dress properly. If I demand that, it becomes my responsibility."

"Well," Emily said, trying to stem the sudden image of dollar bills floating in her head, "I'm sure you'll find someone who'll be delighted to grab the job."

A muscle in his jaw knotted.

"I am sure I shall."

Emily nodded. So did he. Then he stepped into his office. This time, the door shuddered when he slammed it shut.

"Jerk," she muttered.

Did he really think he could bribe her into working for him? Just because $100,000 a year was more than she'd earned in her entire time in New York, just because it would feed and clothe and house her for the foreseeable future, just because she'd be able to tell Lissa and Jaimie about this job, just because even her brothers would be impressed…

She took a deep breath. Expelled it. Thought *no, yes, no…*

Time to stop thinking.

She rapped her knuckles against the door, and then flung it open. Marco was standing at the huge wall of glass behind his desk, his back to her, hands tucked into his trouser pockets.

"You're fired," he growled.

"You can't fire me before you hire me."

"You?" he said, turning toward her. "I thought you were my temp."

"She's probably hiding in the supply closet."

"One laugh after another," he said coldly. "Well, what is it? Did you forget something?"

Emily touched the tip of her tongue to the center of her bottom lip. He wondered whether she knew she did that—and if she had any idea it drove him out of his mind.

"One hundred and fifty," she said.

Marco raised one dark eyebrow.

"One hundred fifty thousand dollars a year. Holidays and sick leave, of course. Health insurance. Six weeks' paid vacation. A review at the end of six months. If you're not satisfied with my work, I get three months' severance pay. If you are satisfied, I get a title—Special Assistant, Vice President, something like that. And a twenty-five thousand-dollar raise."

He narrowed his eyes. "Are you telling me you'll take the job?"

"What does it sound like?"

“One hundred and fifty thousand dollars is a lot of money.”

It surely was, especially since she’d failed at every job she’d ever held, but why tell him that?

Emily gave what she hoped was a take-it-or-leave-it shrug.

“I’m worth every penny.”

They stared at each other. Finally, Marco held out his hand. She took it, gave it a brisk shake, but he didn’t let go. What now? Was she supposed to engage in a silly tug-of-war?

“Eight tomorrow morning. Charles and I will pick you up.”

She nodded. His gaze swept over her.

“Don’t bother packing more than a handful of things. You’ll need to shop.”

She felt her face burn. “If what I wear doesn’t suit you—”

“Do you have cocktail gowns? Evening gowns? Whatever women call those things.”

Emily pictured Jessalyn the night before. The gorgeous dress. The little jacket. The shoes that cost at least two months’ rent.

“No,” she said coldly. “I don’t.”

His smile was as cool as his voice. “As I said, don’t bother packing too many things. A corporate credit card is a perk of the job, remember?”

“Fine. But *you* remember something, too.” Color swept into her face again but her eyes stayed steady on his. “This is business. There won’t be any—any personal nonsense.”

He wanted to laugh. Was that really what she thought had happened between them?

“It isn’t funny,” she snapped.

He nodded. “No. It is not.” His hand tightened on hers. Slowly, he drew her toward him. “So we need one last thing beyond the handshake.”

She read his intention in his eyes but it was too late. A second later, his arms were hard around her and his mouth was on hers.

Her hands came up. She fisted them against his chest.

He gathered her closer.

Warmth cascaded through her blood.

Desire blossomed in her breasts, her belly.

She rose to him, leaned against him, gave him her mouth.

An eternity later, he raised his head. Her eyes opened, looked into the infinite night of his.

"We agreed." Her voice shook; she hated herself for it. "No personal—"

"We did. But I never walk away from unfinished business." His heartbeat was rocketing but it meant nothing. Why would it? The only thing special about this woman was her list of skills. "I kissed you. You kissed me. And now, now what happened is over. It is *finito.*"

The phone rang. Marco let go of her and reached for it. "Frederica," he said pleasantly, "how are you? Yes, I was going to call you…" Talking, smiling, he looked over at Emily and gave an imperious wave of the hand.

Dismissal, pure and simple. Such arrogance! She could almost feel her blood pressure rise.

"No," he said into the phone, "this is a fine time to call. I was just ending a conversation with an employee."

Not just dismissal. Dismissive dismissal, and never mind the stupid redundancy. Better that than the four letter words flooding her brain, especially when she never used four letter words. Well, hardly ever. As for foreign curses—they didn't count.

The man brought out the worst in her. But he was going to lift her out of poverty. Six months. If she couldn't tolerate him after that, goodbye and good luck.

"So, how have you been, Frederica?"

Emily turned her back, marched from the office and

closed the door behind her, although "closed" was too benign a description for a door she slammed hard enough to make her wince.

Someday, she thought grimly, someday Mr. Arrogance would go too far. Somebody would leave his office and shut the door hard enough so that it fell off its hinges.

On the other side of that door, Marco jumped at the cannon-like bang of wood against wood.

He sank into the chair behind his desk.

"Sorry, Jane. No, I realize now that it's you. We, uh, we must have had a poor connection."

Had he come to a decision about Emily Madison? Jane Barnett wanted to know.

"I have," he said.

And wished to hell he understood what, exactly, it was that he had decided.

# CHAPTER SEVEN

The apartment was empty. Nola had left a note propped up on the kitchen counter.

*Had to leave right away. Not to worry. Rent paid. Will keep in touch. XOXOXO*

Emily sighed and put the note down. She'd send her share of the rent to Nola as soon as she received her first paycheck. Right now, she had things to do. Leave a message for the silent-movie buffs, telling them that she wouldn't be available if they needed her. Locate her passport. Pack. Yes, but what did you pack for a trip to Paris?

Paris? Had she actually agreed to accompany Marco to Paris? Maybe the better question was, had she actually agreed to work for him?

He was going to pay her a lot of money.

That was the good news.

The bad news was that she didn't know a thing about him or his company or what a personal assistant or an administrative assistant was supposed to do. Why hadn't she asked?

"Not smart, Emily," she said briskly. "Really. Not terribly smart."

She needed advice but where to get it?

Not from Caleb. He was a lawyer and lawyers saw things in black and white. From Jake, maybe. He ran *El Sueño*. He'd know all about what a PA was supposed to do. Or Travis. He ran his own financial empire…

Brilliant.

Ask one of her overly-protective big brothers about the job she'd agreed to take and he'd cut straight to the chase, find out that she was going away with a man she'd just met.

Forget that.

Nola had worked in offices but Nola was on a tour bus someplace between New York and Timbuktu. Lissa? No good. She'd never worked in an office. Jaimie? Yes! She'd worked at an accounting firm before she'd decided her future wasn't in Excel but in real estate. And Jaimie was smart about life. About men.

Emily checked her watch. Jaimie was in D.C. That meant she was in the same time zone as New York. She grabbed her cell phone and hit a speed dial button.

Jaimie's phone rang. And rang. And…

"Em?"

Emily let out a sigh of relief.

"You're there."

"I'm here. But I'm, um, I'm kind of busy."

"All I need is five minutes."

A pause. Then Jaimie sighed. "Give me a second."

Jaimie must have put her hand over the phone. Emily could hear only bits and pieces. A man's voice. Then Jaimie's.

"… my sister. Of course it is. Why would I say…"

"Jaimie?"

More whispering. Then Jaimie was back.

"Sorry," she said briskly.

"Everything OK?"

"Yes, fine. What's up?"

Emily hesitated. "It's complicated."

"Yeah. Life generally is."

"Hey, I'm the one who studied philosophy, remember? But you're right. Life is complicated. And this…"

This what? What was she going to say? That she'd accepted a job anyone sane would kill for—just as long as you left out a few small details, starting with the fact that she had no idea what the job called for and ending with that kiss?

"Em. Honey, I hate to rush you, but—"

"Fine. Right. Of course. I just thought, you know,

we'd talk, have some coffee…"

It had become a ritual, having coffee or tea while they Skyped or talked on the phone. Anything to make it feel more as though they were in the same room.

Jaimie sighed. "You're right. Let me get something. Maybe a glass of wine…?"

"Excellent. I'll get one, too."

Emily put down the phone, hurried to the kitchen alcove, opened the joke of a fridge and peered inside.

Yogurt. Cottage cheese. Milk. Leftover Chinese. Leftover Thai. Leftover something that looked like a biology experiment gone bad.

Wine. Wine…

There. Half a bottle of cheap Chardonnay. She grabbed it, bumped the fridge closed with her hip, snagged a water glass from the drainer on the sink and poured an inch—what the hell, poured two inches of the pale gold liquid, hurried back to the sofa and grabbed the phone.

"James?"

"Yes. What took you so long?"

"Sorry, sorry." Emily took a healthy swig of the Chardonnay. "So, how've you been?"

"Emily. You called me."

"So?"

"So, something's up."

"Why should something be—"

"Because it is. I can tell. You just called me 'James.'"

"It's your nickname."

"It only became my nickname when you or Lissa had a math problem you couldn't handle."

"That's not—"

"Remember the year you took calculus? I was James before every exam."

Emily sat down, sighed and drank a little more wine.

"OK. I have a problem."

"Somehow," Jaimie said dryly, "I'd bet it doesn't have anything to do with math."

Emily laughed. "See? That's one of the reasons I called you. You're so smart!"

"That's me, all right. Smart."

"Jaimie? Is this a bad time? You sound, I don't know, weird."

"Just tell me your problem. Let the genius go to work."

"OK." Emily cleared her throat. "I have a—a decision to make."

"About?"

"I got a job."

"A real job? Damn! Sorry. I only meant—" Jaimie sighed. "Look, Lissa and I figured it out months ago. You don't really work for a private art collector."

Emily thought of arguing. Instead, she moaned.

"No. I don't."

"See, one of Lissa's friends was in New York. She met you once… Anyway, she was at Bloomie's to buy mascara because she'd forgotten to bring hers and she was pretty sure she saw you working at the Dior counter."

Hell. Emily tried for casual. "She could have said hello."

"Lissa had told her you lived in New York, that you were working for a rich guy with a private art stash."

Emily winced. "Don't tell Travis or—"

"We're your sisters, Em. Not the cops. And there's nothing wrong with selling makeup."

How about playing piano in a bar? Emily thought, but she didn't say it.

"So, tell me about this new job. Is it at a museum? A gallery?"

"Not exactly."

"Then where?"

Emily raised the glass to her lips, frowned when she

found it empty. Back to the kitchen, snatch the bottle of Chardonnay from the counter, tuck the phone between shoulder and ear, fill the glass…

"Em? Where are you going to be working?"

"It's not a where, it's a who. I mean, it's with who. With whom."

"Someday," Jaimie said with a little laugh, "I'm going to murder Jake. Just because he's the grammar maven doesn't mean the rest of us have to be. So? Are you going to explain?"

"I took a job as a personal assistant."

"A personal trainer? But you—"

"A personal *assistant*. A PA. An administrative assistant."

"Got it. To who?"

"To whom."

"Jesus, Em… Fine. To whom?"

"A man."

"Well, that narrows the field."

"His name is Marco Santini. Owns his own company, makes buckets and buckets of money."

"Like Travis."

"I guess. But he's in construction, not finance. "

"And?"

"And, I'm not sure I should have taken it. The job."

"Why?"

"Well—well, I'm not really a PA. I don't do shorthand."

"Except for court reporters, who does? What else?"

"I'm not even sure what a PA does."

"Didn't the headhunter who sent you to this Santini guy give you a description?"

"I didn't go through a headhunter."

"The agency, then. Didn't they—"

"I didn't go through an agency, either. "

"You applied online?"

"No."

"Then, how'd you get the job?"

Emily licked her lips. It was a good question. Too bad the answer wasn't.

*I met him when I was standing in the rain after I was fired from the bar where I played piano.*

"Emily?"

"I, uh, I went to apply for a different job. The woman who interviewed me looked at my application and thought I'd be a better candidate for PA than for the job I'd applied for."

"I assume Santini interviewed you, too."

"Yes."

"Well, what's the problem? If the interviewer thinks you're right, if the guy you'll be working for agrees, why question it?"

Why, indeed?

"Em?"

"Well—well, I really don't know him."

"How could you? You just started working for him."

"Actually, I haven't. Not yet. My first day is tomorrow."

"So you'll know more after that."

"Right. Right."

"Emily? Is there more to this than you're telling me?"

"What more could there be?"

"I don't know. You tell me. Is this guy unpleasant?"

"No."

"Is he dirty? Does he smell?"

*Only in the best possible way.*

"Em?"

"No. No, he doesn't smell."

"Did he do anything inappropriate?"

*He kissed me. And I kissed him back. Does that count?*

"Emily. Can you hear me?"

"No. Nothing inappropriate."

"Then, what's the problem?"

*The problem is that he's self-centered and oh so sure of himself and I know that's not the end of the world but wanting to climb into bed with him probably is not a good thing.*

Oh God. Was that the truth?

"Emily? Emily? Hello?"

Emily gulped down the rest of the wine.

"Yes," she said, "yes, I'm here."

"Are we on the same page with this or is there something missing?"

"No," Emily said with blithe assurance. "Why would there be something missing?"

"I don't know, Em. That's just the point. Why would there be—and how come it sounds as if there is?"

Emily uptilted the glass, recovered the final two drops of wine with the tip of her tongue.

"Just give me your opinion, OK? Should I take the job?"

"How's the pay?"

"Excellent."

"The bennies?"

"Terrific."

"Then why all this second guessing?"

True. Completely true. Why all this second-guessing?

"Em. Honey. You never give yourself enough credit. You're smart. You're talented. Take the job. If it doesn't work out, so be it."

So be it, Emily thought as she sat on the stoop outside her apartment building at 7:45 the next morning.

A job was just a job.

Marco Santini was just a man.

That she found him attractive meant nothing. Especially when, mostly, she found him irritating.

*Be ready at eight.*

A command, not a request.

*Don't bother packing more than a handful of things.*

Another command.

And then that last Directive From On High, delivered like an edict. *I kissed you. You kissed me. And now, now what happened is over. It is finito*.

At least he was right about that.

What had happened was over. Of course it was because, really, nothing had happened. A couple of kisses. Big deal. A night's rest, a little time to think, and she'd realized that.

He'd caught her off guard, was all. Caught her when she was vulnerable, first saving her from the rain and the possible dangers of the street, then offering her a job anyone with a functioning brain would kill for.

The Knight Errant.

Except, he wasn't.

He was accustomed to being the king. What did that make her? A peasant? Be ready at eight. Fine. Not a problem. He was her boss. He had the right to tell her when the workday began. But he had no right to tell her things were or were not *finito* when she had already decided that for herself, and he had no right to tell her what to pack or rather what not to pack.

Emily looked at her suitcase, standing beside her. Nola had once described it as the third room in their two-room apartment.

OK. So it was… large. What good was a suitcase if it wasn't?

This morning, it was stuffed to the brim. Marco had said he would pay for the special clothes she'd need for formal work-related functions. Not a problem there, either, but the clothes she wore every day would be her own.

Right now, she had on jeans, sneakers, a T-shirt, a cashmere cardigan left over from her college days. They were flying to Paris. Well, this is how she'd have dressed if she were flying there alone. For comfort, not for style.

He'd undoubtedly show up in one of those custom-made suits. So what? She would change when they reached the hotel. She had suits. Blouses. Shoes. Everything she could possibly need.

The Knight Errant. Sir Arrogant. He would surely not approve but that was not her problem, it was his.

Actually, his arrogance was his problem.

Emily snorted.

Carrie Bradshaw had Mr. Big.

She had Sir Arrogant.

The thought made her laugh. What a perfect title! Sir. Arrogant. Not Marco Santini, CEO. Not Marco Santini, Employer. Not Marco Santini, Studly Hunk…

Because he was. A studly hunk. How come she hadn't mentioned that to Jaimie?

"Woof!"

Something rubbery, wet and cold jabbed at her hand.

Emily looked down. The owner of the something rubbery, wet and cold looked up. It was a small gray mop of a dog with bows in its hair, polish on its nails, a nose that sniffed at everything nonstop, and the desire to pee on the entire world.

Like her suitcase.

"No," Emily said firmly.

The Mop bared its teeth. The gesture, combined with the bows and polish, turned it into a virtual clone of its owner, Emily's downstairs neighbor and the premier neighborhood gossip, Mrs. Flynn.

The dog inched closer to the suitcase.

"Forget it," Emily said, shooting to her feet and grabbing the case by the handle. Not that that would help. She'd had to bump the thing down the stairs.

"Precious only wants to mark his territory," Mrs. Flynn said.

"The suitcase is my territory."

"Then you have no right to leave it where… Oh my! What-is-THAT?"

Emily followed the woman's stare.

"That" was Sir Arrogant's limo, pulling to the curb. Last night, it had looked big. By daylight, it was the size of a yacht.

The little dog woofed and trotted down the steps with Mrs. Flynn hanging on to the end of the leash.

The rear passenger door opened. Marco stepped from the car.

Mrs. Flynn gasped.

Who could blame her? Emily thought, as her mouth went dry.

He was, in a word, spectacular.

Not in a suit.

In jeans, a dark blue T-shirt, an open leather bomber jacket and scuffed leather boots with a light early-morning-I-forgot-to-shave stubble on his jaw. The jeans were faded; they clung to his narrow hips and long legs. The T clung to his chest and flat belly.

He was a fantasy come true, and if her pulse beat any harder, surely he would hear it.

"Good morning."

His voice was early morning, too, rough and low and husky.

Emily's heart jumped.

So did her libido.

Who was she kidding?

She'd nailed the truth last night. Of course she wanted to climb into bed with Marco Santini. Reality was that she'd climb into the back of the limo with him. She'd climb into anything with him, anything, anywhere, anytime…

"No."

She stared at him in horror. Had she spoken her thoughts aloud?

She hadn't.

Sir Arrogant had delivered the quiet command to The Mop just as it lifted a skinny leg against the limo's front tire. The dog looked at him, lowered its leg, tucked its ratty little tail between its hindquarters and scurried back toward Mrs. Flynn.

Emily looked at Marco. He raised an eyebrow.

Laughter bubbled in her throat.

"You are," she said, "very good at giving commands."

He grinned. "So I've been told." His gaze moved over her, slowly, from the top of her head to her toes and then back up again. "Ready for travel, I see, *cara*."

"Where are you and this—this charming gentleman going, Emily?"

It was Mrs. Flynn. Until that moment, Emily hadn't thought the woman knew her name.

Marco gave Emily a quick wink.

"And who is this delightful woman, Emily?"

"This is—she's my neighbor."

"Catherine. I'm Catherine Flynn," Mrs. Flynn said breathlessly.

"Caterina. Such a lovely name." Marco smiled. "Emily and I are on our way to Paris, Caterina."

"To—to—"

"Paris," Emily said, what the hell, getting into the spirit of things.

"Oh, my," Mrs. Flynn whispered.

Marco went up the concrete steps and eyed Emily's suitcase.

"I can see you followed my directions," he said wryly. "About not packing many things."

It was as good a time as any to establish how she felt about being given orders.

"I'm not always good at following directions," she said sweetly.

He grinned again, hoisted the suitcase as if it were weightless and handed it off to Charles, who stood at polite attention on the curb.

"Are you ready, *cara*?"

The *cara* seemed to sizzle.

"Ready," Emily said.

He reached for her hand.

"Good," he said softly. "So am I."

He brought her hand to his mouth, pressed a light kiss to her palm and closed her fingers over the kiss.

How could she feel that kiss straight to the tips of her toes?

The last thing she saw before the Mercedes pulled into traffic was Mrs. Flynn staring after them, her hand plastered to her heart.

"Honestly," Emily said, swinging around to face Marco, "that wasn't—"

He was laughing. "It was. I suspect we made Caterina's day."

How could she not laugh, too?

"How about her entire year?"

"She is an annoyance, yes?"

"She complains about everything. Last week, she said we'd left the water running in the basement. There's a washer and dryer there, and an old sink, but—"

"We?" he said, his smile suddenly tight.

"I have a roommate. Had a roommate. Nola."

"Nola."

"Yes. And—"

"Is there no man in your life?"

Such a quick change in conversation. And in the way he was suddenly looking at her. That same feeling came over her again, as if there weren't enough breathable air between them.

"No. There isn't."

He reached out. Caught a strand of her hair.

"You left your hair loose," he said softly. "I like it this way."

"Marco. We agreed—"

He nodded. Drew back. "Yes. You're right. What about Nola?"

"What about…"

"Nola left the water running."

"Oh. No. She didn't. I didn't. There was a puddle by the sink but it was probably from Mrs. Flynn's dog."

"A pee puddle," Marco said solemnly.

Emily laughed.

"A canine protest. Against foolish owners dressing them up with ribbons and polish and things that are undoglike."

Emily laughed again.

"That is nice," he said.

"What is?"

"Hearing you laugh." His smile tilted. "I have the feeling you have not laughed enough in your short life."

"That's not true. I mean—"

"I can see that things have not been easy for you, Emily." His voice was low, his eyes dark and serious. "Playing piano in a bar, living in a building like that—"

"Marco," she said quickly, "really, my life hasn't always been—"

"*Si.* I am sure you have some good memories."

"Yes. I do. What I mean is—"

His phone rang. He cursed softly, took it from his pocket and checked the screen.

"I must take this, *cara.* Give me a minute, please."

Emily nodded. Marco began speaking in rapid French. It was about business, a financial deal he was making. After a few seconds, she tuned out.

He thought she was poor. That she'd come from poverty.

She knew she ought to correct him.

*I'm not poor at all,* she'd say. *My family has money. Lots of it. I was raised in luxury and maybe that's why I'm so determined to make it on my own, or maybe it's because I've never really accomplished anything in my life. Either way, you're wrong about me…*

"So," he said briskly, "I have something for you."

She blinked. He'd ended his call. In his hand now was a duplicate of his iPhone.

"From now on, this is yours. All of my contacts are programmed into it. There is no need for any phone."

Emily rolled her eyes.

Sir Arrogant was back.

And that was probably a very good thing.

****

He had a private jet. It waited in the general aviation parking area at Kennedy Airport like an enormous silver bird.

A small, pleasant-looking man met them, shook hands with Marco and with her.

"Emily, this is Jim Bryce. Our first officer. Jim, this is my assistant, Ms. Madison."

"It's Emily," Emily said.

Bryce smiled and asked for their passports. Emily had a bad moment when she realized the name on hers was Wilde, not Madison, but Bryce didn't so much as glance at them.

"I'll have these cleared in a couple of minutes, sir," he said.

Security and customs procedures were different for those who flew in private planes. She'd almost forgotten that.

Charles boarded with their luggage; Marco took her elbow as they climbed the stairs to the cabin door.

"This is Leslie. Our flight attendant." The flight attendant, elegantly groomed, smiled at her. "Leslie, this is my administrative assistant. Ms. Madison."

"It's Emily," Emily said again, holding out her hand. "Nice to meet you, Leslie."

The man standing behind the attendant was the captain, Kier Tate. More smiles, handshakes and introductions all around.

Marco's hand remained cupped around Emily's elbow.

It was a simple gesture. Polite, nothing more—but his fingers seemed hot against her skin as he led her deeper into the cabin.

"There's nothing to be nervous about," he said softly, his lips at her ear.

"Why would I be nervous?" Could it be the feel of his hand? The warmth of his breath? The realization that she was leaving her own world and entering his?

"Surely, you're not nervous about being with me."

"Of course not," she said quickly, whipping her head toward him. Big mistake. His head was still bent to hers. One more inch and her lips would touch his cheek.

He smiled. It was a bone-melting smile.

"If it is because this is your first flight on a private plane, I can assure you that we meet—we probably exceed—all standards."

He certainly exceeded all standards.

As for flying on a private jet… Should she tell him that she had three brothers? That they owned private planes the equal of this? That she had flown with Jacob and Caleb and Travis dozens of times, that she had a friend, Laurel, whose husband, His Royal Highness Sheikh Khan ibn Zain al Hassad of Altara, owned a jet that had taken Emily and her sisters to Altara for a visit last summer?

No.

None of that had anything to do with her as Marco's new assistant.

The truth was, the less anyone knew about her and her background, the better. Even Nola knew very few of the details--only that she had brothers and sisters and that she'd grown up in Texas—because she'd met Nola after she'd decided to stop being Emily Wilde and start being Emily Madison.

One thing you learned when you came from a

wealthy, powerful family was that some people saw you not as a person but as a curiosity.

Sometimes, it was harmless.

Sometimes it wasn't, especially if you were trying to make it on your own.

That had been her experience, anyway.

Coming East had meant a new start.

Here, she'd imagined that Wilde would just be a name. She wouldn't be the youngest daughter of a general, the kid sister of three amazingly successful brothers. She wouldn't be one of the three Wilde girls, certainly not the one who was having the most trouble following in those almost-impossible-to-fill footprints.

She wouldn't be one of the wealthy Wildes—she'd simply be herself.

What a foolish dream!

Her very first interview had been for a fancy-sounding position at a private museum: Assistant to the Curator for Pre-Columbian Art. Once the interview began, she'd realized the job title should have been Gofer for the Pre-Columbian Art department but she'd been cool with that because you had to start a career somewhere.

Things had gone well until the curator took a second look at her résumé.

"You're from Wilde's Crossing? You're one of *those* Wildes?" A big smile had spread over his face at her reluctant nod. "Small world, isn't it? I worked at the Dallas Museum of Art a few years ago. I have some investments with your brother, Travis. Well, that makes me feel a lot better."

At first, she hadn't understood. Then he told her what her salary would be. She couldn't have bought groceries with it, let alone pay for a roof over her head.

"I can't live on that," she'd said politely.

"That's what I mean," he'd said, chuckling as if they'd shared a grand joke. "You won't have to. You're a

Wilde!"

Not two nights later, she'd gone to dinner with a nice enough guy who'd taken her out a couple of times before. That evening, out of the clear blue sky, he asked her where she was from.

Without thinking, she'd said she was from Wilde's Crossing.

"Huh. The town's named after your family?" he'd said.

She'd tried to recover fast, told him that it could be.

The next time he saw her, he called her Poor Little Rich Girl. He'd Googled Wilde's Crossing, Googled her. Hell of a thing, he'd said, almost angrily, that a girl with all her advantages would play at being poor.

Lesson learned.

Emily wouldn't play at being poor, she would be poor. That was when she'd dropped her last name. Just let it sail away, like a helium-filled balloon rising into the sky. Her middle name, Madison, gave her the anonymity she needed and it felt comfortable because it already belonged to her. She'd retyped her résumés and contacted her college, had them add a note to her files so that if anyone called to verify her transcript, she'd turn up as Emily Madison as well as Emily Wilde.

And that was it.

She wasn't a Poor Little Rich Girl anymore; she was simply another girl scrambling to make it in New York.

That was how Marco saw her. Emily Madison, on the search for a good job and an interesting career, and if he wanted to believe he was introducing her to a lifestyle she'd never known before, how could she tell him she knew all about the way people with money and power lived and do it without telling him more about herself than he needed to know? He'd hired a Madison, not a Wilde, and that was the way things would remain.

Nothing personal. It had to do only with business.

So when he reassured her about the safety of private

planes, she smiled politely.

"Thank you. That's good to hear."

What wasn't reassuring was the way her breath caught at the feel of his hand on her waist, the hardness of his body as she brushed past him toward a soft leather chair.

"OK?" he said.

Emily nodded. "Fine."

"Good." He cleared his throat as he sat down in a chair angled toward hers. Charles had disappeared behind a door at the rear of the plane. "I know this is all very sudden. This job. This trip. You must have questions."

"Lots."

"For instance?"

"Well, what are my responsibilities? Who works with me? Do I report directly to you?"

"Good questions. Let me answer them one at a time. You report only to me. You work only with me, although there are times various of my managers will work with you—or perhaps I should say, through you. You will be their conduit to me."

Emily looked at him. "I bet they won't like that."

"Some won't because you are new to them. It will be part of your job to convince them that they'll be better served following the protocol I've set up. As for your responsibilities… they will be far reaching. You'll take notes. Organize them. Read reports and break them down to ten pages instead of a hundred. You'll attend meetings with me. Be my eyes and ears during the kinds of events where everyone is intent on pleasing the boss and hiding the truth."

She sat back. "You expect a lot."

"I expect my one hundred and fifty thousand dollars' worth."

His expression gave nothing away. She could only hope hers didn't, either.

"And how do you know I can do all these things

adequately?"

"I don't. I'm taking a gamble on it, *cara*." The muscle in his jaw flickered. "That is one of the things I am good at. It is one of the reasons I am where I am today."

Emily sat up a little straighter. "And if your guess is wrong?"

He shrugged. She thought of a big cat out on the veld, acknowledging the remote possibility that it might have misjudged the fleetness of a gazelle.

"If I am, then we end our relationship at the six-month mark."

"Six months to prove myself," she said softly.

"Six months to prove we were made to be together," he said, even more softly.

She wanted to look away from him. She couldn't. She did the next best thing and took the conversation in a direction that would clarify what they were talking about.

"Did your other assistants all live up to the standards you set?"

"One, years ago."

"Oh."

His lips curved in amusement.

"Her name was Beatrice. She was sixty-five, a grandmother who decided her granddaughter needed her more than I did."

"Oh," she said again, and felt her pulse blip.

"I've had assistants with management degrees, advanced degrees, complex office experience, everything that looks good on a résumé."

"And?"

"And, they didn't work out." He hesitated. For the first time since she'd met him, he looked… uncomfortable. "Some of them seemed to imply that I am…difficult."

"No."

"Yes. It has been suggested to me that…" His eyes

narrowed. “Are you laughing at me?”

“Would I do that to my boss?”

His gaze moved over her face. She was definitely laughing at him. When was the last time someone had done that? People did not laugh at him. For the most part, they didn’t even laugh with him unless they were very, very sure it was what he wanted them to do.

She was an enigma, this new assistant.

Beautiful. Bright. Tough. Tender.

And kissable. Eminently kissable, which was certainly not anything that would look good on a résumé, he thought, his eyes narrowing even more until they were all but hidden under the sweep of his dark lashes.

“I don’t know exactly what you would do to your boss,” he said in a low voice. “Perhaps you would care to enlighten me.”

“Don’t,” she whispered.

He reached out. Ran his thumb over her mouth. She felt her lips part.

“Don’t what?” he said, just as softly.

“Don’t flirt with me. This is business. You said—”

“Sometimes,” he said, curving his hand around the nape of her neck, “sometimes I say the damned stupidest things.”

“Marco—”

“Emily,” he said, and then his mouth was on hers.

The kiss was long and deep. She heard herself make a little sound, felt his hands close on her shoulders. He drew her to him; her breasts pressed against the hard wall of his chest. He said something in Italian; one of his hands threaded into her hair. The other rose and cupped her breast.

Her nipples budded; he groaned as the one he was caressing stabbed into his palm.

A little burst of static filled the cabin.

“We’re next for takeoff,” the captain announced over the loudspeaker. “Seat belts, please.”

Marco raised his head. Emily raised her lashes, opened her eyes, saw that his were wide and black with passion.

"Seatbelt," he said gruffly.

He rose and walked away.

Three hours later, the flight attendant served lunch.

"Just coffee, thank you," Emily said, and heard Marco, several seats behind her, say the same thing.

Except for passing him on her way to the bathroom, she didn't see him again until the plane touched down at Charles de Gaulle Airport almost six hours later.

# CHAPTER EIGHT

They went through Customs together, all of it very businesslike.

"My assistant," Marco said briskly, when the customs officer looked at Emily and then at her passport.

Try to remember that, she almost told her new boss, but she smiled politely as the officer returned the passport to her.

Charles met them at the curb, seated behind the wheel of a shiny black Bentley.

Bentleys. Mercedeses. Her brothers used cars like these, too. Why did it bother her that Marco did?

She knew the reason.

He was Sir Arrogant. All those hours of the flight, thinking about how he'd kissed her, as if it were his right to change the rules because he was the person who'd established them—

"A limo for every city?" she said, her tone sweet to the point of nausea.

Marco settled into the leather seat beside her, picked up a slim leather case and opened it.

"No," he said, "only when I don't drive myself."

She looked at him. "Very amusing."

"Since it obviously bothers you—"

"Why would it bother me?"

"Since it does, and since you'll be the one dealing with the expenses for the automobiles I own and rent, I will explain."

"You don't owe me an explanation. You're the boss."

Marco looked at her. "Yes. I am," he said pleasantly. "And, as such, I see a need for larger cars on occasion. Tonight, for instance."

"What about tonight?"

"We are having dinner with a CEO and his wife. I doubt the four of us would fit comfortably in a Porsche or a Lamborghini, which are normally my vehicles of choice. And just to put you at ease about the Mercedes, I drive a Ferrari when I'm home."

"Home."

"Yes. When I am in New York. Satisfied?"

"No."

*"Dio!* What now?"

"You said 'we.' When you talked about tonight. What does that mean?"

"How easily you forget, Ms. Madison. You are my assistant. Of course, I said 'we.'"

Emily's thoughts flew to the clothes in the suitcase Charles had loaded into the Bentley. She went through them all. Went through them again.

Somehow, she doubted that her best black suit, fraying a little at the cuffs, would do for a Bentley, a Frenchman and his French wife.

"I have nothing to wear," she said, and winced at how clichéd that sounded. "What I mean is—"

"I know what you mean. That clothing allowance."

"Yes. And obviously, I haven't had time to—"

"To shop." Marco opened the leather case. "That's all taken care of."

"Taken care of how?" Emily leaned over. "Is that an iPad?"

"It is your iPad. I'm just making sure that everything you need has been loaded onto it... Good. Excellent. There are notes about Monsieur Rogan and his wife here, in this file. Be sure and look at it after you dress."

He closed the iPad case and handed it to her. She put it in her lap.

"After I dress in what? I just told you, I haven't shopped."

"And I told you that is taken care of."

"How?"

"You'll find a couple of suitable outfits in our suite."

"What? You shopped for me?"

He raised one dark eyebrow. "Not me. I phoned the concierge. She picked up some things."

"You did this without consulting me?"

"What was there to consult about?"

Emily stared at him. He sounded genuinely baffled.

"How about checking to see if that was OK, for starters?"

"You just said you have nothing suitable to wear."

"Well, yes. But—"

"I repeat, what was there to consult about?"

"Well…well, color. Size. Style."

"Sapphire blue. Or a somewhat paler shade."

"Did it ever occur to you," Emily said coldly, "that I might not like blue?"

He shrugged. "It is a good color for you."

"Your opinion, but I—"

"Your eyes are blue. Sometimes they are dark, like an angry sea. Sometimes they are light, like a mountain sky early on a summer morning."

His voice had gone low and husky. Her gaze flew to his. Something hot and electric flashed between them.

She felt a flutter low in her belly.

"That's not…" She swallowed. "That's not a good reason for—for—"

"It is an excellent reason."

Arrogant. He was so damned arrogant!

"As for the size…" His tone was casual again, the voice of the master dealing with a servant. "I described you. The concierge thought a size six."

"I'm an eight," Emily said. "See? You're not always… What do you mean, you described me?"

Another shrug. "Height. Shape. I described you and she said six and I said that sounded right."

"Was Jessalyn a six?" Emily said, and could have bitten off her tongue.

His smile was slow and sexy.

"Jealous, *cara*?"

"Certainly not. I just wondered how you could make that determination so easily."

"I have not lived my life in a monastery."

No. She was sure he hadn't. Who knew how many Jessalyns had been in his life, how many would continue being in it now that he was free?

"So, there will be a dress. A gown, actually. Shoes. The necessary accessories."

"I'll probably pop out of the dress and have to scrunch my toes to get into the shoes," Emily said, and he, horrible and arrogant man that he was, laughed.

They rode in silence for a few minutes. Then she opened the iPad, found the notes he'd left for her and began to read through them.

"There's a lot here," she said. "Didn't you think of filling me in while we were in the air?"

He glanced at her. That telltale muscle in his jaw knotted as he turned away, stared straight ahead and folded his arms over his chest.

"I should have done so but my thoughts… took a detour."

There were endless answers to that but she wasn't foolish enough to try and lay the blame for what had happened on him. He'd kissed her, yes, but she'd been more than a willing accomplice.

Even the thought sent heat shimmering through her blood.

She was in deep trouble.

"*Cara.*" The sweet endearment sounded exactly like a caress. "Your face is an open book."

"Don't call me that."

"Still," he said softly, "it is true. I can read what you are thinking."

"Has anyone ever told you that life isn't all about you and what you can and can't do?"

Those amazing eyes of his darkened.

"Has anyone ever told you that you are a puzzle a man would find challenging to solve?"

She wanted to tell him he was being ridiculous, that a woman would never be moved by a line as corny as that.

But she couldn't.

She couldn't because what she really wanted to do was ask him if he meant it, if she could be a challenge for a man like him

"Emily," he said, and the only thing that saved her from making a fool of herself was a tangled knot of typical Parisian traffic, a blast of French car horns, and thank heaven for that sudden dose of reality.

****

The City of Light was as beautiful as she'd remembered.

She'd been a teenage kid the last time she'd visited Paris. She, Jaimie and Lissa had spent a couple of weeks of summer vacation with the general on one of his European command tours.

They'd stayed in his assigned housing, an impressive apartment near the Arc de Triomphe, and he'd seen to it that their days were filled with carefully escorted tours. Still, they'd found the occasional chance to sneak away and wander along the Seine or pop into the McD's on the Champs-Elysées, where Lissa, the eldest at fifteen, would try to look old enough to order beers with their Big Macs and *frites.* She never pulled it off but it was the trying that counted.

They'd also attended a couple of formal functions including a dinner the general had hosted at the George V, one of Paris's most elegant hotels. Well, not the dinner. The cocktail party before it. They'd worn velvet dresses: Emily's had been the color of rich summer grass.

"Circulate among my guests and make me proud of you," had been their father's command, which had meant show them that you can make useless conversation in French as well as in English.

Lissa had slipped off and somehow charmed her way into the kitchen to watch the sous chefs at work. Jaimie had wiled away the time doing complex math problems that involved the number of guests and the number of canapés—something like that, anyway.

Emily had dutifully chatted with half a dozen people and then she'd wandered into an adjoining salon, discovered a beautiful piano and spent the next few minutes happily playing Chopin until the general found her.

"So it's *you* making all this noise," he'd said sharply. "It's carrying through to the next room. You are not a pianist, Emily. Remember that."

Such a foolish thing to think of on her first day in Paris in more than a decade. Things had changed. She was an adult now, here as assistant to a man who had chosen her for that position because he believed her capable of handling it.

*Yes,* a voice inside her whispered, *but are you, really? You've failed at so many other things…*

"Emily?"

Marco spoke softly but the sound of his voice still made her jump. He frowned and put his hand over hers.

"What is it, *cara*?"

"Nothing. Really. I was just—I was just thinking of the last time I saw Paris."

He smiled; his hand lifted to her face and cupped her cheek.

"Isn't that a line from an old song?"

She wanted to turn her face and kiss his hand. It felt so right against her skin. Warm. Comforting. And wasn't it crazy that his touch could be comforting when only hours ago it had been exciting?

Wasn't it more than crazy that a man she hardly knew should have the power to affect her this way?

"Emily. Tell me what you are thinking."

His voice was low. Thick. She looked at him and felt it again, that rush of electric excitement.

"I don't know," she whispered, because suddenly lying was impossible. "That's the problem, Marco. I don't know what I'm thinking."

He made a sound halfway between a groan and a growl. Slowly, he lowered his head to hers and kissed her.

It was a soft, brief kiss, the simple whisper of his mouth against hers. She could have turned away.

But she didn't.

She let the kiss go on and on.

In the end, it was Marco who took his lips from hers.

His eyes were the color of the night.

And she thought, *oh God, I could fall into those deep, dark pools and drown.*

****

They made the rest of the drive into the city in silence.

Say something, Marco told himself.

An excellent idea—but what should he say? Should he apologize for kissing her? No. How could he do that when, dammit, he didn't regret that kiss, didn't regret any of the kisses they'd shared?

That last kiss, especially. The sweetness of it. The tenderness.

No apologies—even though kissing her was a mistake.

He'd meant what he'd told her in his office. He did not mix pleasure with business. Not ever. A business dinner, no matter how elegant, was all about business. A game of tennis or golf played with a rival was business.

Every decision of his adult life had been made with business in mind, even before he'd had his own business to run.

It was how he had gotten to where he was today.

Emotion was emotion. Logic was logic. A man who mixed the two was a man asking for trouble.

Another lesson learned from his brief marriage.

Marco shifted his weight as the Bentley entered the city.

Sex. Desire. Those were provable things. They were measurable. They had their place, and it was not the office.

Back to square one.

He had made a mistake, hiring a woman he found desirable.

It was too late to do anything about it now. He needed Emily's services on this trip, but as soon as they got back to New York…

"We're here, sir."

The Bentley had pulled into the semicircular drive of the hotel. His hotel. La Boîte à Bijoux.

He smiled.

If there was anything it was safe to be emotional about, it was a building like this.

****

Emily had spent the trip from the airport telling herself that she should quit her job before it all blew up in her face.

She'd worried about being in over her head as far as the responsibilities of it were concerned. What she hadn't considered was that she was in over her head in terms of—what could she call it except her libido?

She wanted a job, not an affair. She was bad enough at keeping jobs; she could never keep a man. Not that she'd ever tried, but a man like this…? She wasn't cut out for one night stands or one-week stands or however long the Marco Santinis of this world could be expected to find a woman… what had called her? An interesting puzzle.

If he only knew.

There really wasn't anything puzzling about this. Pared down to basics? She wanted to sleep with the boss.

In other words, it was time to go home.

Only one problem.

She'd agreed to work for him for six months. Was that an oral contract? Even if it was, she could break it… and that led to the second problem.

Where was she going to get the money to fly home?

Dammit, this was the borrow-to-pay-the-rent thing all over again. She couldn't turn to her brothers, couldn't go to her sisters...

"Emily."

Could she stick it out for just a couple of days? They wouldn't be here very long…

"Emily."

She blinked. The car had stopped. The door was open. Marco was standing outside, holding out his hand.

"We've arrived," he said.

She nodded. Pushed her hair back from her face. Took his hand because it was the polite thing to do and…

And, where were they?

She hadn't really thought about it but if she had, she'd have figured they'd be staying at the George V or the Plaza Athénée. Where else would a man like Marco Santini stay than in one of the city's famous hotels?

This building wasn't a hotel she'd ever seen before. She reminded herself that she hadn't been in Paris in a very long time.

A semicircular drive. A building made of gray stone. Bright blue awnings. Flower boxes filled with yellow chrysanthemums. And a doorman who beamed from ear to ear as they approached a set of wide brass doors.

*"Monsieur Santini! Bienvenue!"*

Marco ginned. *"Bonjour, Cristoffe. Comment allez vous?"*

*"Bien, monsieur, très bien."*

Marco put his hand lightly in the small of Emily's back.

*"Cristoffe, c'est Madame Madison. Elle est mon aide.* Emily, this is Cristoffe. He is—"

*"Bonjour, Cristoffe,"* Emily said, and she and the delighted doorman chatted in French while he opened the doors to a lobby that was as charming as it was handsome, done in polished wood and gleaming marble floors.

The staff greeted Marco like an old friend; he introduced her and everyone nodded and smiled and shook her hand before a bellman led them to a cage of brightly polished brass, the kind of elevator she'd always associated with Paris.

It took them to the tenth floor.

The doors opened directly onto the lounge of their suite.

The bellman who'd accompanied them assured them that their luggage would arrive shortly. Marco thanked him politely, discreetly handed over a tip that made the man's smile even wider, and waved him out.

"Well?" Marco said, once they were alone, "what do you think?"

What did she think? Emily walked slowly through the lounge, skating one finger over an ormolu clock, brushing her hand lightly across the back of a beautiful Louis XIII chair. He didn't know it, of course, but she'd been in a lot of upscale, elegant hotel suites—and this outshone them all.

"I think—I think this is absolutely beautiful. What's the name of the hotel?"

"La Boîte à Bijoux."

"The Jewel Box. Oh, that's perfect!"

He nodded, his gaze wary, his answering smile hesitant.

"Is it new?"

"It went up four years ago."

She walked to a pair of French doors that gave onto a small terrace enclosed by window boxes filled with more bright yellow chrysanthemums. A pair of wicker chairs were drawn up to a round table topped by a glass-enclosed candle and a small vase that held yellow roses and tulips.

Beyond, the Eiffel Tower rose against a perfect blue sky.

Emily stepped onto the terrace. She turned toward him, her face bright with pleasure. "What a wonderful place!"

His smile became a little more certain.

"The terraces are my favorite part. There are two more, one off the master bedroom and another off the dining room. Because of the way the suite was constructed, there's a 360 degree view of Paris. The tower. The Arc de Triomphe. The Palais Royale…" He gave a small laugh. "Listen to me. I sound like a travelogue."

"You sound like a man who understands how lucky people are to stay in such a beautiful suite. I can imagine who does stay in it. Kings. Princes. Presidents."

"Actually," he said, color creeping into his face, "I am its only occupant. The suite is mine."

"Really?"

Marco smiled. How little it took to make her happy, he thought, and heard himself say what he had surely not intended to say.

"Actually, the entire hotel is mine. I built it."

Her eyes widened. With shock? No, he realized. With delight.

"I designed it, too," he said because, what the hell, why not go for the bottom line?

"You mean the furnishings?"

"*Dio,* not that! Did I want armchairs? Slipper chairs? What does a slipper have to do with a chair?" Emily laughed and he laughed along with her. "What I designed was the building. It was an easy step. I'd become more and more interested in the planning of structures, not just putting them up, so when I started thinking about expanding my company, I decided to take a deep breath and—"

"And?"

And, what? What was he doing?

The details were surely boring to anyone but him

The hotel had begun as a one-shot, a practical way to establish his corporate name in the commercial heart of a great European city, but somewhere along the way, he'd found himself taking an interest in it that went beyond schematics and cost projections.

Now, he had other boutique hotels on the drawing board. The industry knew about MS Enterprises' new venture, but he'd kept the depth of his involvement private.

A man made himself vulnerable if he made the mistake of letting people know more than was necessary about him.

"And?" Emily said again.

Marco cleared his throat.

"And, I'm pleased with how things turned out."

She laughed. "Come on, Marco. Pleased? You must be delighted."

"Well," he said cautiously, "well, yes. I guess you could say that."

"Absolutely, you could say that." She threw her head back, drew in a long breath of air. "I'd forgotten the smell of Paris," she said softly. "Old, wonderful, so lovely."

Lovely, indeed.

Her sculpted profile. The graceful line of her throat. The glint of sunlight streaking her hair, not loose as he would have wished it but at least only barely constrained today in a flowing ponytail.

Desire twisted inside him. Hunger. And something more.

The feeling stunned him. He caught his breath.

Then he caught his sanity.

"We're running late."

Emily looked at him. The expression of delight on her face faded. He wanted to take back his gruff words, wanted to tell her that he wasn't angry, that he was, *Dio,* that he was a man standing on some kind of precipice.

Instead, he looked at his watch as if it held the answers to all the mysteries of the universe.

"Very late," he said, even more gruffly. "The bedrooms are down the hall. The one with the pale pink walls will be yours."

He'd hurt her by being so abrupt; he could see it in her eyes.

"The clothes I mentioned… they'll be in your dressing room."

"I'll need things from my suitcase."

"It will be here shortly, but as I already told you, what you will wear this evening is in your dressing room."

So much for her eyes showing hurt. What they showed now was anger. Good. He could deal with her anger. It was her other emotions that were a problem.

"Thank you for making all these decisions without consulting me."

"We had this discussion on the plane. There was no need to consult you. I provide you with a clothing allowance, remember?"

"But not with your choice of clothing. *You* remember *that* in the future."

Oh yes, she was definitely angry. That flash of fire in her eyes. That tilt to her chin. It made him want to go to her and pull her into his arms, kiss her until she clung to him, until neither of them could tell where he ended and she began.

Her door slammed. She was good at slamming doors, he thought, and almost laughed.

Instead, as slowly as if he were a man twice his age, Marco sank into a chair and put his head in his hands.

He had made a mistake. Forget the old bromide about never mixing business with pleasure.

Even more true was what he'd realized from the start. Emily didn't belong in his life. Perhaps it was more accurate to say that he didn't belong in hers.

What had just happened, her open show of joy at something as simple as the terrace instead of asking endless questions about where they were dining, how many Michelin stars it would have, the name of the celebrity chef, the famous people they might see…

How could such an innocent survive in his world? How could the superficiality of it not affect her?

Yes, he wanted to take her to bed. And he could do it. The cold truth was that he knew women, knew how to read the little signals they gave.

Emily melted against him when he took her in his arms.

She sighed when he kissed her.

The sweet little whimpers she'd made during those few moments on the plane when he'd touched her breasts…

He could have her on her back in less time than it took to think about doing it.

She would be sweet and she would be shy; she would learn what he wanted from her, what he wanted to do to her, what he wanted her to do to him. She would learn, and turn to flame, and their affair would be like none he'd ever known.

And then he would end it.

He was meant for mistresses.

Emily was a woman meant for one man, one love,

forever.

Marco shot to his feet, paced to the terrace, stepped onto it and stared out over the soot-stained old chimney pots of Paris.

He had been wrong to hire her. To bring her here.

He would send her home.

As far as an assistant was concerned… he could manage. He could contact the offices he had in Milan. Surely, they had someone on staff who could fly here and do the job. Or he could contact a French employment agency and hire a temp. Neither solution would be ideal; he had no way of knowing if Milan or an agency would send him someone who was competent but the truth was, he still didn't know the degree of Emily's competence, either.

He only knew that he had to put her out of his life, the sooner the better.

Marco checked his watch again.

It was too late to telephone Milan, too late to seek out an employment agency. And he had a dinner engagement in, *Cristo*, in forty five minutes.

Quickly, he walked down the hall.

His bedroom adjoined hers.

He stepped inside, slammed the door—hell, one good slam deserved another—peeled off his shirt, toed off his mocs, yanked off his jeans and boxers.

His tux—well, one of his tuxes—was hanging in the dressing room. He kept hotel suites in several cities, each stocked with whatever clothes he might need. Life was simpler that way. More efficient. It was a plan he had worked out years ago.

He strode into the bathroom, turned on the multiple sprays in the glass-enclosed shower.

Emily, on the other hand, would have two gowns to choose from. Which would she pick? He'd made arranging for the clothes sound easy. In actual fact, he'd spent almost an hour on the phone, first with the concierge, then with the personal shopper she'd contacted at a shop on the Rue de Rivoli.

"I want a dress. No. Two dresses. Also shoes, handbags, whatever is necessary, delivered to my suite," he'd said briskly.

But briskness had turned to confusion in a heartbeat. Did *monsieur* want morning dresses? Afternoon dresses? Or did he want gowns for the evening? Colors? Fabrics? And the shoes. Pumps? Sandals? Strappy sandals?

Strappy sandals? What in hell were strappy sandals?

The consultant had explained. She had also explained heel height. And, she'd added, would *monsieur* wish undergarments as well? Yes? Of what type? Lace? Silk? Full bras? Demi bras? Waist cincher corsets? Thongs? Bikinis? Panty hose? Thigh-high hose?

"Thongs," he heard himself say. "Bras to match the thongs. Lace. Silk…"

He'd fallen silent.

"Monsieur? Are you there?"

No. He wasn't. He was in a place he wasn't supposed to be, and he'd opened his eyes, rubbed his hand over his forehead.

"Whatever you think is appropriate," he'd said gruffly.

Then he'd ended the call, his body one hard, endless knot of sexual frustration, his head filled with images of Emily in stilettos, a silk thong, sheer stockings.

And nothing else.

The same image was in his head now. Her bathroom adjoined his. He could hear the water in her shower beating against the marble floor. Another picture replaced the one in his head.

Emily, naked.

Beautiful.

High, tip-tilted breasts. Slender waist. Hips just right for his hands to grasp as he brought her body into hot contact with his.

And her face. That exquisite face. Blue eyes, liquid with desire as they met his. Rosy lips, parting as he brought his mouth to hers.

He saw himself draw her closer. Felt the silkiness of her nipples against his chest, the press of her pelvis against his belly.

His hands were in her hair, all that dark gold spilling over his fingers.

Her arms were around his neck as she lifted herself to him.

He groaned again, head falling back as he all but heard her cry of pleasure as he entered her, filled her, felt her heat close around him…

*"Merda!"*

Marco shuddered. His eyes flew open.

He had just disgraced himself in a way he had not done since he was a boy.

Shaken, he quickly turned all five shower heads to cold. Gasping, he lifted his face to the icy spray.

Tomorrow, first thing, he would make the necessary arrangements for a new assistant and then he would send Emily home. No. He would send her home, then make the calls. That way, he would not leave himself any possible reason to keep her here. He would pay her a month's salary. Two months'.

The only thing he had to do was get through tonight.

Surely, he thought as he shut off the water and reached for a bath sheet, surely he was man enough to do that.

# CHAPTER NINE

The gowns Emily found in her dressing room were… the only suitable word was stunning.

There were two, both made of silk. Long, slithery things that would skim her body, curve at her hips, follow the long line of her legs right down to her ankles.

One had sleeves. One didn't. Not that it mattered. Both would leave her shoulders bare and her cleavage displayed.

And they were expensive.

Incredibly expensive. She'd have known that just by looking at them, even if they hadn't hung in garment bags that carried the name of a shop any woman who'd ever read Vogue would recognize.

How ironic.

She had a closet full of expensive things at *El Sueño*. Not as expensive as this but expensive enough. She'd deliberately walked away from that life of extravagance, a life her father had insisted on and funded.

Now she was immersed in it again.

Yes, but this was different.

This wasn't the general demanding that everything about his daughters be a positive reflection of him, his wealth and his status.

This was her employer requiring that his employee be properly dressed for a business function. He hadn't been involved in choosing the gowns or the shoes, the evening purses or the two elegant little jackets, one of soft silver leather, the other of gold satin, hanging beside the gowns.

He'd made a phone call to the hotel concierge and she'd taken it from there.

There was nothing personal in any of this.

Only the underwear made that conclusion

questionable.

The lingerie. No way could you call such tiny bits of lace and silk underwear. The bras, the thongs, the sheer hose were the stuff of dreams. Hot dreams.

Emily swallowed dryly.

Trust a French concierge to make choices like these. Because it surely could not have been her employer. He wouldn't have asked for bras and thongs that made a woman think about a man slowly taking them off her.

A rap sounded at the bedroom door.

"Fifteen minutes," Marco called.

That brusque tone did it. If she'd had any doubts as to who had chosen the lingerie, she didn't any more.

Five minutes later, he knocked again. Pounded, was more like it.

Emily was ready.

Her suitcase had still not arrived, but the gorgeous marble vanity offered shampoos, soaps, body lotions, perfume, every possible little luxury, and she'd had lip gloss, mascara and a tiny sample thingy of eyeliner in her handbag. What she didn't have was a hair clip.

When she opened the door, she was holding her hair back from her face with one hand.

"You don't have to break it door down," she said, "See? I'm—"

She never got to the "ready" part.

She was too busy staring at her boss.

His hair, still shower-damp, curled silkily against his head. His face was freshly-shaven. He was wearing a black tux, and if ever a man was made to wear a tux, this was the man.

He stared at her.

It was impossible to read his expression.

"You look," he said, his eyes focusing on hers, "you look…"

What? Awful? Dreadful? Good? Bad?

"For God's sake," she said, "say something! Should

I have worn the other—"

"Beautiful."

His voice was low. Husky. He sounded exactly the way a woman wanted a man to sound when she'd dressed just for him.

Except, she'd reminded herself quickly, except she hadn't dressed for him. She'd dressed for a dinner meeting. And he wasn't a man. She wasn't a woman. He was her employer. She was his employee.

"Thank you," she said, a little breathlessly. "It's the gown. The shoes. It isn't—"

"But it is," he said softly. "It is you, Emily. You are beautiful."

Time seemed to do that thing everyone knew was impossible.

It stood still. And then, just when she thought she was going to tumble forward on these impossible, delicious heels and drown in Marco's eyes, his cellphone rang.

His face darkened.

He wrenched the thing from his pocket, barked "What is it?" so harshly that she felt pity for the unfortunate soul on the other end.

He listened, nodded; his expression eased. When he disconnected, whatever had happened a moment ago was over.

"Charles is waiting."

"Oh. I mean, good. I mean, I'm almost—" *Stop babbling, Emily! He's calm. You should be, too.* "I just need to find something for my—"

"*Dio,* will you please stop fiddling with your hair?"

Maybe he wasn't as calm as she'd thought. No matter. She didn't like his tone of voice.

"I beg your pardon?"

"I said—"

"I heard what you said. I am not fiddling with it, I'm fixing it. I'm trying to figure out a way to secure it because my suitcase still hasn't arrived and I don't have a barrette or a band and—"

"It won't arrive."

"What won't arrive?"

"Your trunk."

"It's a suitcase."

"It felt like a trunk." Marco folded his arms. "And it will not be coming."

"Why not?"

He shrugged. Unfolded his arms. Examined his fingernails.

"I have informed Charles to return it to the plane."

Emily's eyes narrowed.

"I beg your—"

"If you say 'I beg your pardon' one more time," he said in a low voice, "I will show you the only sure way you can beg me for whatever it is you want, *cara*."

The warning flustered her. It also put a lick of flame low in her belly and she didn't want to think about why that should have happened.

"Mr. Santini—"

He laughed. She blushed.

"Marco. That is my luggage. It holds my clothes. My—my stuff. You had no right—"

He waved his hand. Louis XIV could not have done it with more arrogance.

"Tomorrow, we buy you new clothes."

"Tomorrow, we buy you new clothes," Emily mimicked. "What are you talking about?"

"Do not mimic me. And do not look at me that way. The clothing allowance, remember?"

Emily let go of her hair. It was her turn to fold her arms. "You probably spent all of it already."

"I spent what needed to be spent."

"Really?" Her chin lifted. "You know, you never did tell me the amount of that allowance."

"I did not tell you the amount of your health

insurance, either."

"It isn't the same thing."

"It is what I say it is—and why are you arguing with me?"

"Does no one ever argue with you?" she snapped. "Because someone should. You are the most—"

"The most arrogant man in the universe. *Si.* You told me that before. Perhaps you have forgotten that Charles is waiting. So are my guests."

"Well," Emily said, grabbing for her hair again, "they'll just have to—"

"*Madre de Dio*, stop that nonsense with your hair!"

He caught her wrist. Her hair tumbled to her shoulders and down her back.

"See what you've done," she said crossly. More crossly than the situation warranted, and for what reason? Why was her heart racing? Why was she so aware of his closeness? Of the scent of man and soap? Of the heat of his hand on her flesh? "I cannot possibly go to an important meeting looking like—"

Marco cursed, hauled her toward him and silenced her with a kiss.

She went crazy.

She moaned. Cupped his face between her hands.

He made an answering sound, deep in his throat, wrapped his strong arms around her and gathered her tightly against him.

Her lips parted.

Their tongues met.

She sucked the tip of his into her mouth.

He growled, slid one hand down her spine, cupped her bottom and lifted her into him.

His erection was swift, hard and exciting. She felt its urgency, felt the urgency of her response.

She began to tremble.

Then he let her go.

She blinked her eyes open.

His face was taut with tension, the bones visible beneath his tanned skin.

"This isn't going to work," she whispered.

"No," he said thickly, "it isn't."

He reached for her. She went into his arms. Their mouths fused. The kiss was deep and hot and she had never experienced anything remotely like it.

His phone rang. And rang.

She flattened her hands against his chest.

The phone went on ringing.

Finally, eons later, Marco raised his head. Emily stepped back.

He took a long, shuddering breath. Concentrated on snow. Ice. Glaciers. Why wouldn't his damned body cooperate? At last, it did. He was safe to be seen in public.

"Time to go," he said.

Then he took her elbow, as impersonal a gesture as a gesture could be, and led her to the elevator.

****

They were seven for dinner.

The CEO of the French company Marco was interested in buying. His wife. An accountant from that company. An accountant from Marco's Milan office. A middle aged woman the CEO introduced as his *assistante de direction*.

My counterpart, Emily thought, smiling as she and the woman shook hands.

The CEO's PA wore a probably expensive but dull-looking black silk evening suit. It had a mannish jacket that topped a long, straight skirt. Sturdy black shoes peeked out from under the hem.

Emily's peacock-blue silk gown was, she knew, spectacular. Her shoes had all the substance of a spider's web, the slender heels five inches high.

One of them, she thought wryly, was not suitably dressed.

The restaurant where Marco had booked a private room had three Michelin stars and was rumored to be on the verge of getting an all but unprecedented fourth.

It was world famous and elegant.

Emily had been here during that decade-old visit she, Jaimie and Lissa had paid to their father.

"The obligatory paternal visit," Jaimie had called it, and she was right.

They all hated those pilgrimages. To be fair, now that Emily was older, she knew their father really had wanted to spend time with his daughters. The trouble was, he didn't know how to do that without making them feel as if they were on display and as if everything they did was a reflection of him.

The meal here, a luncheon, had not gone well.

Their father had ordered for them. Poached quail eggs. Lissa had rolled her eyes. Bretagne oysters. Jaimie had turned a gag into a cough. Frogs' legs. Emily had shuddered.

In fact, their palates were sophisticated.

It was their behavior that wasn't.

They were hormonal as thirteen-fourteen-and fifteen-year-old girls can be, filled with the need to assert themselves to a father who did not believe that children could or should be assertive.

He had spent the morning reminding them that they were to be on their best behavior. Lissa was not to play with her hair. Jaimie was not to swing her feet under the table. Emily was not to speak before thinking. She had a bad habit of doing that.

It had been all but inevitable that something truly awful would happen that day.

It had come in the form of a seemingly simple question.

Midway through the endless lunch, one of the

general's distinguished guests, a much-beribboned French officer, had smiled at them the way some adults smile at children. To call the curve of his mouth under the shadow of a bristly mustache "condescending" would not have come close.

"Well," he had said, "after all these days of dining on our glorious French food, mes *jeunes filles,* what is the very best dish you have eaten?"

The general had beamed at them.

They had looked at each other, meaningful glances that translated into a pact of incipient teenage rebellion.

"Speak up," their father had said. "Jaimie? Lissa? Emily? Emily. Tell us your favorite French dish, child. What is it, hmm? *Blanquette de Veau? Cassoulet? Pot au feu?*"

Defiance had glinted in Emily's eyes. She thought of where the three of them had spent a guilty hour that afternoon.

"Big Macs and *frites*," she'd replied.

Back home, that might have gotten a laugh but not here, in the gastronomic capital of the world.

Their father's face had turned purple.

"My daughter has an unusual sense of humor," he'd said.

The only good thing that had come of the incident was that he'd sent them home the very next day. It had also earned her praise from her sisters and cheers from her big brothers after Lissa told them the story.

Thinking back, she found herself trying not to smile.

"What?" Marco said softly, dipping his head to hers.

She looked at him, wanting to share it—but she couldn't.

For the first time, she let herself think about how she'd lied to him, if not directly than surely indirectly. It was a textbook example of guilt by omission.

He thought she was struggling to get ahead.

She was struggling to leave her old life behind.

He thought he was expanding her world. That, at least, was true, but not in the ways he believed.

"Emily?"

He took her hand under the table. She looked into his dark eyes. Her stomach dropped to her toes.

Forget that he thought she was someone she wasn't.

The real problem was what she wanted to be, the woman he took to his bed.

The lyrics from one of those old songs she used to play at the Tune-In floated into her head.

*Bewitched, bothered and bewildered...*

In other words, she was in deep, deep trouble.

****

Miraculously, she got through the rest of the evening playing the role of knowledgeable administrative assistant.

She listened. Committed to memory things she thought Marco might want to consider later. Quietly translated an occasional word or two when it seemed important to do so. And when the business portion of the evening ended, she smiled and exchanged pleasantries with the others.

At last, chairs were scraped back and handshakes were exchanged. Air kisses from the French CEO and his wife for her, a second set of air kisses from the CEO's wife for Marco, a friendly slap on the back from the CEO.

A deal had been cinched.

Then they were in the limo and Charles was taking them back to the hotel.

"Well," Marco said, smiling, "that went very well."

Emily looked at him. "You think?"

"I know. You did an excellent job."

She breathed out a sigh of relief. "Thank you."

"For what? It is the truth." He grinned. "The

Frenchman said that if ever I decided to part with you, he would hire you in a heartbeat at twice whatever I'm paying you."

She laughed. "You don't think it's dangerous to tell me that?"

His smile tilted. "I think that everything about you is dangerous, *cara.*"

She felt her pulse skitter.

"Not to worry," she said lightly, deliberately misunderstanding what he'd just said and the smoldering look that was suddenly in his eyes. "I'd need all kinds of fancy documents and permits to take him up on his offer."

"I would not let that happen."

His voice was low, his expression intense. It didn't take a genius to know they weren't talking about documents and permits.

He reached for her hand. She caught her breath as he stroked his thumb over the delicate skin on the inside of her wrist.

"Don't."

He answered by taking her hand in his and bringing it to his lips.

"Please…"

"Please, what?" he said in a husky whisper.

"Please—please stop. This isn't a good idea."

His eyes searched hers. That muscle in his jaw knotted.

"Emily…"

She shook her head, tugged her hand free.

She didn't want this.

All right. She wanted it and that was exactly why it was a bad idea.

Marco was her employer. One benefit of having held zillions of jobs was that you knew from the dubious pleasure of firsthand observation that a disaster resulted when a woman slept with her boss.

More to the point, did she want to be just another in the string of women who passed through his life? No matter that Jessalyn was a bitch. Did she want to end up like her, dumped without any concern for her feelings?

Even if that didn't happen for weeks, even a few months, was it better than a hookup?

Besides, she knew how these things worked.

She'd watched how her handsome, arrogant brothers had dealt with women in their bachelor days; she'd listened to her sisters rant and rave and sometimes sob when errant lovers broke their hearts.

"Emily," Marco said again, the urgency in his voice so real she could almost see it, just as Charles pulled the Bentley to a stop at the hotel.

She reached for the door handle. Charles got there first. Beyond him, the night doorman held open the door that led into the lobby.

Door after door lay ahead.

The one to the private elevator. The one to the suite.

The one to her bedroom.

It had a lock. She would turn it, take off this beautiful gown, the so-sexy-they-made-her-ache bra and thigh-high hose and thong. She'd put on—What?

She didn't have her suitcase. That meant no sweats. No PJs. No oversized T-shirt. Comfort clothes, all of them. There was a bathrobe in the sumptuous bathroom. She'd wrap herself in it, climb into bed and sleep until morning.

Then, in the light of the new day, things would be simpler to define.

Marco followed her out of the car, through the door, through the lobby and into the elevator. She stared straight ahead as it rose; she felt his eyes on her but she wasn't going to turn toward him.

The door slid open and they stepped into the suite. Moonlight seeped through the terrace doors and windows and dappled the marble floor.

“Goodnight,” she said, and started down the hall.

Marco came after her. He clasped her shoulders. She closed her eyes. She could feel herself starting to tremble.

“No,” she whispered, but he was already turning her toward him, slowly, slowly, his hands warm on her skin, his eyes, when finally she was facing him, so dark and deep that just looking into them made her feel breathless. “No,” she said again, but even as she said it, his arms were closing around her and she was turning her face up for his kiss.

# CHAPTER TEN

Emily had said "no."

She'd said it twice.

He had not imagined it—but now she was in his arms. Her face was turned up to his. Her lips were parted, her breathing erratic. He could feel the race of her heart against his chest.

Still, a gentleman would have hesitated. A gentleman would have asked, "Are you sure?"

But he was not a gentleman.

He had never been one, not really. What he was now—a man who owned homes on two continents, and an island and a plane—was what the world saw.

Inside, where it counted, he was still a street kid who'd grown up poor and damned near homeless; he was a guy who'd fought no-holds-barred battles to get where he was today.

So, no.

He wasn't a gentleman.

That was his secret.

He dressed like one. He lived like one. The hand-tailored suits and handmade shoes. The elegant homes. The Ferrari, the Mercedes, all the cars, all of it.

Elegant on the outside.

Lean and hungry on the inside.

It was the reason he went after whatever he wanted without hesitation. He knew, he had always known, that no one would simply give him what he wanted.

He had never wanted anything, any woman, as he wanted Emily.

He was a man on fire, in desperate need of possessing her, and he took her mouth with a hunger that had been building inside him from the first moment.

She made a little sound.

Protest? *Dio!*

Despite what he was, who he was, he had never taken a woman who didn't want him. If he had to let her go, if he had to stop kissing her…

It wasn't a whisper of protest.

It was a sweet, soft cry of need and he groaned, took her face in his hands and changed the angle of the kiss, took it deep, deeper until the taste of her flooded his senses.

She slid her hands under his jacket, felt the thunder of his heart against her palms.

He wrapped his arms around her, his hands cupping her bottom, and lifted her against him.

She gasped at the feel of his erection pressing against her.

He told himself to slow down. He was out of control, going too fast. Much too fast. He *had* to slow things down.

But how could he?

Her tongue slid against his. Her hips rocked against his. Her arms locked around his neck; her head fell back and he buried his mouth in the hollow of her throat, tasted the dampness of her skin, felt the throb of her pulse beneath his lips.

"*Cara,*" he said, his voice low, hot, dangerous. "*Cara mia,* wait."

She stiffened in his arms. "Don't you want this? Oh God, Marco, I didn't—"

"I want this more than I have ever wanted anything. But—"

"But?"

"But you deserve more. I don't want to hurt you."

She made a sound that might have been a laugh.

"The only way you could hurt me would be if you stopped."

Her words sent a shudder through his body.

He lifted her higher. She wrapped her legs around

his hips. He felt her dress ruck up, felt the hot core of her against him. One big hand cupped her bottom; his fingers spread, curving over her thong.

She gasped.

He muttered one raw, potent oath and tore the scrap of silk away.

She whispered something as his hand swept across bare skin, satin smooth, silky, hot.

So hot.

Not just there.

Here, he thought, closing his eyes as he moved his hand between her thighs. *Dio,* she was hot here, as well. And wet. So wet…

He parted the soft folds of her femininity. Found the bud that flowered within. Closed his eyes as she shuddered and cried out.

She was responsive to his every caress. So responsive that he had to grit his teeth and fight what he felt welling inside him. Could a man come just from this? From the taste of a woman's mouth, the scent of her arousal, the sound of her cries?

He had always prided himself on his control. In business. In sex. In all aspects of his life. Where was that control now? He was a man standing at the edge of a cliff, knowing that once he launched himself into the unknown, there might not be a way back.

Slowly, he told himself, go slowly.

He stroked her again, his fingers whispering over her clitoris. She dug her hands into his hair.

"Marco."

Had his name ever sounded so right?

"Marco." Her voice trembled. "Please. Please. Please…"

She moved against him. Against his hand.

His mind blanked to everything but this.

This, he thought, as he reached between them and zipped open his fly.

This, he thought as he stumbled back against a silk-covered wall.

This, he thought, and he drove into her.

She came instantly, her muscles convulsing around him, his name a cry that pierced the silence.

The night spun around him.

"Oh God," she sobbed, "oh God, oh God, oh God…"

He clasped the back of her head and brought her lips to his, kissed her as he rocked into her again and again. He felt the second orgasm race through her, heard her cry his name against his mouth.

He wanted the moment to last forever but it couldn't, it wouldn't; inside his scrotum, his belly, he could feel his own release building, the ultimate essence of life.

"Now," he groaned, and she buried her face against his throat, bit him with the fierce delicacy of a tigress as she came again, as he gave himself up to the whirlwind and exploded inside her.

A final tremor swept through her. Boneless, she collapsed against him and he stood absolutely still, just holding her, feeling her, breathing her in.

After a very long time—an hour, a lifetime—she lifted her head. He kissed her, a sweet kiss that made her sigh.

Slowly, he eased her down his body. Her feet touched the cool marble floor. She swayed and he gathered her against him.

"*Cara,*" he said softly. "*Cara mia.*"

She shook her head. Her hair tumbled forward, hiding her face. Tension gripped his body.

"Sweetheart. What is it?"

She shook her head again. He slid one hand over her cheek. Her jaw. Cupped it, lifted her face to his.

"Don't," she whispered.

His heart constricted.

"Was I too fast? Too rough?"

Another shake of her head. Her hair slid across his fingers, silken and scented. He caught a strand and brought it to his lips.

"You were—you were wonderful."

He felt a little stab of pride at her softly spoken words.

"You are what is wonderful, *cara.*"

"But I—I shouldn't have—" She paused. "I promised myself that I wouldn't—"

"That you would not what?"

"Do… this."

"And what is 'this?'" he said softly.

"Marco. Don't tease me."

"You promised yourself we would not make love."

Ridiculous that his words should make her blush.

"Emily." He put his hand under her chin, tilted it up until her eyes were level with his. "Such a wonderful thing to tell me, sweetheart."

"That I didn't intend this to happen?"

"That you knew that it would happen. No, don't look away from me. You knew. So did I. This was inevitable."

"We're—we're strangers. We've only known each other for three days."

"Four," he said solemnly. "It's past midnight."

He'd wanted to make her laugh. At least he'd succeeded in making her smile.

It made his heart turn over.

Her hair was a tangle of silk. He'd kissed off her lipstick; her mouth was the palest pink and slightly swollen from the demand of his.

He could feel his body hardening again.

She had the look of a woman fresh from her lover's bed and that was where he wanted her.

In his bed.

In his arms.

"You're right, *cara*. We only just met." His mouth brushed hers; she sighed in a way that made him lose his train of thought. "But does that matter? I knew what I felt for you the minute I saw you standing on a rain-soaked street corner. 'Look at that,' I thought. 'Such a beautiful woman and she is waiting just for me.'"

She smiled again. It made his heart flutter with pleasure.

"What you thought," she said, "was that someone had to rescue me. You were my knight. You took pity on me."

"What?" he said in mock horror. "Pity? For a Botticelli Venus, rising from the sea?"

"Some Venus," she said, and when her lips curved in another smile, he used it as an excuse to gather her closer.

"I understand, *Emilia mia*. You are not a woman who makes love with a man she hardly knows."

"Don't," she said again and he thought that if she said this was not making love, it was sex, he would—he would have to repeat what they had just done because she was wrong.

"You make me sound like a—a model of virtue!"

"You are a bright, beautiful small-town girl, making her way in a world that is new to her without succumbing to its temptations."

"I'm not a small-town girl. Not really."

"Dallas is a big city, cara, but it could not have prepared you for New York or the kind of neighborhood in which I found you."

Emily's chin came up. *Dio,* he loved the way she did that, all her determination and independence shown in one small, perfectly feminine gesture.

"Do you have any idea what it's like to be desperate for a job?"

"I know precisely what it is like." His voice hardened. "I know what it is like to have to take work you hate. To sweat and struggle because you have no one to help you. No one who can pay your bills or see that you don't have to worry about putting food in your belly."

"See? That's what I mean about our being strangers. I *have* family. And they would have helped me if—"

"If they could. I am sure that is true, *cara*. But clearly they couldn't."

"You don't understand. My relationship with them is—"

"Difficult? Ah, sweetheart, I am sorry." His hands cupped her shoulders. "But you have me now." His gaze drifted the length of her body; he felt his muscles tighten, his blood start to thicken. "And we have more important things to do tonight than talk."

He bent his head, kissed the place where her throat and shoulder joined. How could a simple kiss be so electrifying?

"That's not fair," she whispered. "You're trying to change the subject."

His laugh was rough and low and sexy.

"I am indeed. Why would I want to talk about anything but you and me and how you look right now? So beautiful. So well-loved—and yet, not loved enough."

"Marco. Please listen to me."

"I am listening." He laid his hand over her breast. "I can feel what your heart is saying, that you need me to make love to you again."

She wanted to deny it but he was right. She needed the strength of his embrace, the heat of his body, the taste of his skin. She wanted him, all of him. It was a wonderful feeling. A terrifying feeling. To give herself over so completely to a man when she had never, ever dreamed of doing something that would leave her so vulnerable, so exposed.

He lifted her face to his and kissed her. She told herself not to respond but, God, the feel of his mouth on hers, the touch of his hands…

"How does this thing fasten?" He turned her so that her back was to him. "Hooks? Buttons? Ah. A zipper."

"You're impossible," she said, so softly, so sweetly that he felt his pulse thud.

"Not wanting to make love to you again is what is impossible."

The gown slid slowly off her shoulders, exposing golden, silky skin. He swept her hair aside, bent his head and pressed his mouth to the nape of her neck.

"I love the taste of you," he said thickly.

And she loved the feel of his mouth on her flesh. The delicate nip of his teeth. She moaned, leaned back against him and turned her head so she could offer him her lips. He captured them with his, swept the tip of his tongue into her honeyed mouth and as he did, he slid his hands inside the gown and cupped her breasts.

Her moan of pleasure sent a jolt of need straight to his balls. He closed his eyes as his fingers moved over her lace-covered nipples.

The front clasp of the bra came apart in his hands and joined the silk thong he had torn away only moments ago.

Her gown began slipping down her body. She caught at it but he clasped her wrists and the gown fell to her waist, her hips, her thighs.

It fell to the floor and pooled at her ankles.

She was naked now.

Almost naked.

All she wore were the impossibly skinny heels and the filmy black stockings.

Marco stood behind her, holding her, still fully dressed. She could feel the faint roughness of his jacket. His trousers. She could feel his erection, hard and demanding at the juncture of her thighs.

Everything about the moment was exciting and erotic. That she was wearing so little and he was wearing so much, that she could feel all that masculine power pulsing against her…

She began to tremble.

"Do you like me to do this?" he whispered, his lips at her ear, the warmth of his breath like flame against her skin. "To touch you like this, *inamorata*?"

His hands cupped her breasts again. There was nothing to separate her warm skin from his caress. His thumbs moved over her nipples, the sensation sharp and exquisite. Could she come only from his touch there? From his teeth clamped lightly in the nape of her neck?

"Marco," she sobbed, "oh God, Marco…"

What she needed, what he could give her, was in her voice. Marco clasped her shoulders. Turned her to him.

And felt a punch of hunger that almost stole away his breath.

She was beautiful. More than beautiful.

The fall of caramel hair. The pale gold skin. Her eyes, all pupil now, looking up at him through a curtain of spiky dark lashes. Her lush mouth, swollen from his kisses. The ripe breasts tipped by pale pink nipples. The slender waist, flat belly and long, long legs.

And yet, most beautiful all was the expression on her face.

Need. Desire. Passion. For him. Only for him.

Marco, the master of control, knew he was close to tumbling her to the floor, parting her thighs and embedding himself deep within her. He would take her again and again until she was beyond thought, beyond reason, beyond anything but wanting him and his possession.

No.

He wanted to give her more.

Slowly, he told himself, *Dio,* do not be a boy, be a man.

His eyes never left hers as he shrugged off his jacket. Toed off his shoes and socks. His hands went to his tie, fumbled with it and somehow, he got it undone. The buttons of his shirt were more difficult. By the time he reached his cufflinks, he was lost. On a low growl, he gave up, ripped them free and tore off his shirt.

Emily's gaze dropped to his chest.

He watched her eyes widen.

And felt his ego expand.

He was not a vain man.

He was muscled and toned, but he had started life as a man who'd built his body naturally through grueling physical work. Once that was behind him, he'd installed gyms in the homes he owned and put them to hard use.

For his health, he would have said had anyone asked, but now he knew, crazy as it sounded, it had been because he had waited his entire life for Emily's eyes on him. For, *Cristo*, for that delicate swipe of her pink tongue over her rosebud lips as she looked at him.

Her eyes on him was a caress.

Slowly, very slowly because now that he was in control of himself he wanted to draw out every moment of what had become the perfect seduction of lovers for each other, he undid his belt. His trousers were unzipped from what had happened before but now he was contained within his boxers and when he kicked the trousers away, he knew that his erection tented the black silk fabric in a way that did nothing to hide his desire.

He watched her face.

He had been inside her.

But she hadn't seen him.

He was big. He knew that. He'd never thought much about it although women had said things to him, appreciative things. But this was Emily. Would the size of him frighten her? Would it please her? Her response to him had been so passionate, and yet there was an innocence to her.

He waited.

Her gaze swept lower.

Color flooded her face.

*Dio!* He could feel himself swelling though he would not have imagined such a thing possible. Any harder, any bigger and surely he would die.

"Emily."

His voice was rough. Her head came up; her gaze flew to his. He reached for her hand, Brought it to him. She made a little humming sound as her palm curved over the fly of his boxers. Her tongue appeared again, a kitten's tongue, and slicked across her bottom lip.

He shut his eyes. Concentrated on—on anything but this. Counted silently to five. To ten…

And almost went to his knees when her hand reached inside his fly and wrapped around his fevered flesh.

He groaned.

She sighed his name.

Her fingers moved against him in delicate exploration. His head fell back.

"Does this please you?" she whispered.

He gave a broken laugh. She started to pull back; his closed his fingers over hers and taught her to let her hand ride him as he would soon ride her.

He was going to come from this, only from this, from her touch but he didn't want her to stop, didn't want this to end…

A shudder went through him.

He clasped her hand and took it from him.

"No more," he said gruffly, "or this will end too soon."

He curved his hands around her hips. Bent his head, Kissed her breasts, teased the sweet pink nipples with his tongue, his teeth. She moaned. Her hands dug into his hair and she moaned again as he drew first one nipple and then the other into the wet heat of his mouth.

He raised his head.

"Do you like when I do that?" he said thickly. "Tell me what you feel."

"Yes. Oh yes. Oh yes…"

"And this?"

His free hand slid between her thighs. A cry rose in her throat as his fingers parted her.

"Don't. Oh, don't. I can't stand it when you—"

His thumb moved over her clitoris. Back and forth. Back and forth. He could feel the soft, delicate flesh swelling under his touch, could see Emily's eyes blur with passion.

He dropped to his knees. Cupped her bottom. Found her with his mouth.

She sobbed his name as he sucked and licked, as took her up and up, into the night, into the star-shot night where she shattered into a million bright crystals.

Her legs buckled.

She would have fallen if Marco had not risen quickly to his feet and swept her into his arms. He kissed her. Deeply. Endlessly. She lifted her arms, wound them tightly around his neck, tasted their mingled passion on his tongue.

"Emily. *Emilia mia,*" he whispered. "I need to be inside you."

"Yes," she said, "yes."

He said something rough, graphic and hot enough to make her bury her face against his throat as he carried her through the moonlit hall to the place she wanted to go, the place where he wanted her to be.

His bed.

# CHAPTER ELEVEN

Emily woke to soft early-morning sunlight streaming through the floor-to-ceiling bedroom windows, turning the white silk walls the delicate pink of a Caribbean seashell.

Marco's arm was around her, holding her close. Her head was on his shoulder; her hand was splayed over his heart.

His face was inches from hers. He was still sleeping, his breathing deep and steady. She could look at him as long as she liked.

He was the most beautiful man she'd ever seen.

His dark hair was tousled. From her fingers, she knew, from her hands digging into those ebony strands as he'd made love to her. His lashes were midnight crescents against the high arc of his cheeks.

Somebody had to pass a law against men having lashes like that.

His nose was straight and strong… Wait. There was the tiniest bump just at the bridge. Her brother Caleb had broken his nose back in his high school days, playing football. The injury had left a bump much like this. Had her lover once broken his nose, too?

And wasn't it amazing that an imperfection could make a perfect thing even more perfect?

Her gaze dropped to his mouth.

She loved his mouth.

Soft-looking in repose. Sometimes tender. Sometimes demanding. Warm. Silken. Passionate against her throat, her breasts, her thighs.

"What are you thinking, cara, to put such lovely color in your cheeks?"

Startled, Emily's gaze darted to his. Those gorgeous lashes were lifted; she could see herself reflected in his pupils.

Caught, she thought, and her blush deepened.

"I thought you were sleeping."

"Mmm." He rolled to his side, swept the hair back from her face with his free hand. "No. I am awake. Most assuredly awake."

His laughter was soft and wicked. The feel of him was wicked, too, hard and aroused against her hip.

"You have a bump on your nose," she said softly, touching his nose with the tip of her finger.

"*Si.* I was working on a stone wall. I used my hammer too hard. A piece of stone flew off. It and I had a disagreement."

She laughed. "And the stone won." She smiled. "I'm trying to picture Marco Santini working on a stone wall."

He captured her finger, drew it into his mouth.

"I am a man of many parts, *cara*."

"Mmm. I know."

He smiled. "Did you sleep well?"

Such a polite question from a man whose hand was moving over her backside, delving lightly between her thighs, doing such wonderful things beneath the duvet.

They had slept hardly at all and he knew it. She'd come awake in his arms twice during the night, dreaming he was caressing her and finding she wasn't dreaming at all.

"I slept very well, thank you."

Her words were prim. Her breathing wasn't. Neither were the little moans she couldn't control as he touched her.

"No dreams?" he whispered, pushing down the duvet.

His eyes swept over her breasts. It was almost as if he were touching them; her nipples budded under his gaze.

"Because I dreamed," he said. "I had some wonderful dreams."

She gasped as he bent to her and closed his mouth around one nipple. The feel of his teeth and tongue was electric. Her body arched against his; her hand rose and cupped the back of his head.

His hand slid over her belly. Lower. Lower. His fingers danced over her labia. She gave a sharp little cry of surrender and her thighs fell open.

"I love the way your body melts under my hand."

He shifted position. She was beneath him now. She loved lying beneath him. Loved the feel of his long, muscled body on hers.

His finger stroked into her.

She groaned.

He shifted position again. Just a little. Just enough for his erect penis to take the place of his finger and lightly kiss her flesh.

She cried out. Her hips lifted; she moved against him. He raised his head—he wanted to see her face as he made love to her—and she whispered "No" and used her hand to urge his mouth back to her breast.

He loved that about her. Her honesty.

He had been with enough women to sense when a moan was more about making the correct sound than about pleasure, when a touch was more about the performance than the emotion.

There was nothing false in Emily's responses to him.

She was lost in his caresses. And he loved the way she gave herself over to him.

Only one difficulty. What she was doing right now, her cries, the shifting of her hips, the feel of her hands on him made him want to drive into her.

He would wait.

He wanted this to be all for her.

The problem was that each time they made love, he forgot that he was a man who watched and waited and never quite lost himself to the woman in his arms. A piece of him always stood outside, a cool observer of the action.

He seemed to have lost that ability.

The proof had come after they'd made love somewhere in the deepest, darkest part of the night.

After, he'd wrapped her in his arms. They'd fallen asleep with him still inside her. A minute, an hour, an eternity later, he'd jerked awake to a stunning reality.

He hadn't used a condom. Not once. He hadn't even thought of it.

He'd stared up at the ceiling, Emily warm in his embrace, telling himself he hadn't just lost control, he'd lost his sanity.

She'd stirred against him.

"What's the matter?" she'd said sleepily.

"I did not…" He'd cleared his throat. "Emily. I did not use a condom."

"It's all right. I should have told you. I'm on the pill."

Relief had flooded through him, but he knew there was more to be said.

"Still, I should have thought—" He'd paused. "You need to know that I am free of disease," he'd said, hating the way passion had succumbed to science.

"So am—"

Marco had stopped her with a kiss. Of course she was free of disease. She was Emily.

And if he had made her pregnant, he thought now, he would have done the right thing. Married her. Raised their child with her. It would have been the right thing. That would have been why he would have done it, the only reason, because marriage or children or even permanence in a relationship was not on the agenda…

Deep, deep within him, some emotion he could not quite identify fluttered its wings.

"What are you thinking?" Emily said softly.

Marco bent to her, captured her lips with his, drew her into a deep kiss that left her breathless and left him aching.

"I was thinking about my dream. Shall I tell you what it was?"

She smiled and put her palm against his jaw. The dark stubble was soft against her skin.

"Yes."

"I dreamed of you," he said in a low voice. "Just like this. All golden hair and creamy skin. I imagined you in my bed, wanting me as I wanted you."

Her heart beat picked up, became a staccato beat at the dark edge in his words. When he cupped her breast and teased her nipple between his fingers, she could feel that edge of danger in his touch.

"You're always so sure of yourself," she heard herself whisper. "What if you were wrong about me wanting you?"

The look in his eyes sent a wave of honeyed excitement licking along her skin.

"Then I'd take you anyway. I'd ravish you until you begged for mercy." He bent his head, tongued her nipples. "And if you begged, "he said in a rough growl, "I would ignore your plea because you are mine, *inamorata*, to do with as I wish."

*Dio,* what was he doing? Hell, he knew the answer. He was driving them both toward the edge of a cliff. He could feel every muscle in his body trembling and Emily was right there with him, trembling, making incoherent little sounds, lifting her hips so that his swollen penis brushed against her slick, hot skin.

"I was merciless," he whispered.

"How?" she said, so softly that the word seemed to drift on the still air.

"I captured your hands," he growled, curving his fingers around her wrists. "And raised them high over your head."

Her body arched toward his as he drew her arms up.

She cried out.

Her lover's sweat glittered on his wide shoulders and tight torso. His face was that of a conqueror.

She shuddered.

This was torment.

This was paradise.

It was too much.

It was not enough.

Her lashes fell to her cheeks. A rainbow of light shimmered against her closed eyelids.

Marco's grip on her wrists tightened. He kissed her, his mouth hard and demanding on hers. She returned his kiss with the desperation of a woman who wants everything a lover can give.

When he drew back, she sobbed his name.

"Open your eyes," he said roughly. "Look at me."

Slowly, she did as he'd commanded. Her heart turned over.

She saw his beautiful face, hard-edged with passion; his eyes, opaque black pools that could carry her into an oblivion that would never end.

"Marco," she whispered, and he drove deep into her.

She came instantly, her scream of rapture thin and high, and filled with wonder. She tried to free her hands. She wanted to wrap her arms around him, draw him into the abyss with her, but he wouldn't let her.

"Whose woman are you?" he said, his face a mask of hard-fought control. "Tell me."

She bit his shoulder, tasted salt and sweat and man.

"Yours," she said brokenly.

"Only mine." he said, the words rough with command.

He drove into her again and, God, she shattered, wept as she spasmed around him, bucked against him as the world spun away.

He let go of her wrists. She wound her arms around his neck. He slid his hands under her bottom and lifted her to him.

Together, mouths and bodies fused, they flew into the fiery heart of the sun.

****

After a long, shared shower they dressed casually in jeans, T-shirts and sneakers, and had breakfast on the bedroom terrace.

Tiny strawberries flown in from Africa. Café au lait. Chocolate croissants.

Emily bit into one and reached into her lap for her napkin but Marco leaned across the glass-topped table, caught her hand with his and kissed the tiny smear of chocolate from her lips.

"Just trying to be helpful," he said solemnly.

She smiled. "Such a Boy Scout."

"Trust me, *cara*. I was never a Boy Scout."

"No Scouts in Italy? That's where you grew up, isn't it?"

"*Si.* I was born in Sicily." He lifted his coffee cup to his mouth. "And I suppose there must be Scout troops there but not where I lived."

"Where was that?"

She'd meant, in what town or city, but his answer was more specific.

"I grew up in what you would call public housing. In Palermo."

"Oh."

"Oh, indeed."

"What I meant was… "

"I know what you meant." He shrugged. "And yes, it is a long journey from a slum to this."

There was an edge to his voice. Not defiance, exactly, but something close to it.

"I bet it was an interesting journey," she said softly.

"I am a very private man, *Emilia mia*. I have been asked to tell the story of my life at least a hundred times but it is a story that is no one's business but my own."

She could almost see the wall go up around him. It hurt. She wasn't sure why it should, because he was right—his life was his private affair. Still, after the intimacy of the long night…

"I understand."

A muscle knotted in his jaw. Then he put down his cup, reached for her hand and brought it to his lips.

"No. You do not understand. It has never been anyone's business—until now. I want you to know about me."

"Marco. You don't have to—"

"Italy is different from America. It is all very modern, but under the surface many of the old ways still survive. There is what remains of centuries-old aristocracy. There are those with new money. There is a middle class. Small, but there is one." The muscle in his jaw knotted again. "And then there is what Italians call the *popolino.*"

"The people."

"*Si.*The people. What they really are is the underclass. The poor. The uneducated. I was born to a teenage mother. Her family disowned her when she became pregnant with me."

Emily wanted to take him in her arms but she knew better. Instead, she nodded.

"It must have been a hard life for her. And for you."

He shrugged. "She died when I was small. I don't remember her very well."

"And what happened to you?"

"I lived with her mother and father for a while."

He'd called them her mother and father. Not his grandparents. There was a world of meaning in the way he'd phrased that.

"The state put me there but—but it did not work out. So the state put me into a home for kids like me." His mouth thinned. "That didn't work out, either."

“And after that?” Emily said, while her heart broke for a little dark-eyed boy, all alone in the world.

“I ran away when I was sixteen. Worked odd jobs. I was strong. Big for my age. I saved and saved. Then I landed a job as laborer with a crew building a vacation home for a rich American.”

“The stone wall,” Emily said.

He nodded. *“Si.* I learned a great deal that summer, not just about walls but about America. The American told me he had worked hard at my age, too. He said America was a land of opportunity. He said a man could come from nothing in America and if he worked hard enough, he could become somebody.” Another eloquent shrug. “So I saved my money and came to this country. End of story.”

“Why do I think there’s more to that story than you’re telling me?”

“Ah, *cara,* don’t look at me that way. This is not the sad tale of a boy who led a difficult life; it is the tale of one who saw the chance to change what fate had planned for him and took it.” He brought her hand to his lips again. “I tell you all of this because I want you to know me. Not the Marco Santini the world knows. The real one. The one who still lives inside me. He is a street kid who knows he has to fight for what he wants. And sometimes—sometimes, he is hard on those around him.”

Emily smiled a little. “Is this an apology in advance for the times you’ll turn into a snarling Simon Legree with no patience for errors?”

“Who is this Simon Legree?”

“A character in a book. He was a slave driver.”

“I am never a slave driver...” He sighed. “Are we talking about my temporary PA?”

“You mean,” Emily said sweetly, “the one I never saw because you’d terrified her into running away?”

“I was a little impatient with her. OK. More than a little.” Another sigh. “Very well. I will send her flowers.”

"Flowers are nice," Emily said gently. "A letter thanking her for doing her best would be nicer."

"That's just the point. She did not do her best."

"If you'd given her a chance, she might have."

"You don't understand. There is no room for softness in the corporate world. You want to reach the top, you climb the ladder. And once you are there, you've got to keep moving. You must keep your eyes trained up and never look d—" He paused. *"Cristo,"* he said softly. "I sound like a fool."

"You sound like a man who got to the top and maybe, just maybe, forgot how hard it was to get there."

Marco shook his head.

"You are too clever to be my assistant, *Emilia mia*. Before I know it you will be the one giving orders. All my competitors will want to hire you."

She grinned. "There's an idea."

"But I won't let that happen. I won't let you out of my sight. I don't want you more than two minutes away from me."

"Good. Because I don't want to be more than—"

He leaned in and kissed her. The kiss was long and tender and by the time it ended, Emily was in Marco's lap, her arms around his neck.

"You are a much nicer man than you think you are," she said quietly.

"There are hundreds of people who would disagree with that assessment."

She laughed. "Then they don't know you as well as I do."

His smile faded. "No. They do not. I have revealed more of myself to you than I have to anyone else. Ever." He paused. "I was married once, a very long time ago."

"What happened?"

"We were wrong for each other. I was wrong for her, anyway."

"Do you still—"

"No! I tell you this only because I want you to know the real me, *cara*. And I have never wanted that before, not with anyone."

His admission sliced into her heart. He was giving her truths about himself, and she had given him lies and fabrications.

If there was ever a time to return his gift of honesty with the gift of her own, now was that time.

But what would he think if she did?

"Hey." He touched his forehead to hers. "What's that sad look for? I was not some saintly little kid, sweetheart, if that's what you are thinking."

"No. I wasn't thinking that." She hesitated. "I was thinking how—how important it is for people to know the truth about each other."

"I agree. And now you know the truth about me," he said, waggling his eyebrows. "I am not just a disgustingly rich, amazingly wonderful lover. I am a brilliant self-made man."

It was impossible not to laugh—but there was still her truth to deal with.

"Yes, you are." She dragged in a breath. "Seriously, though—"

He smiled. "You think I am not being serious when I tell you that I am brilliant?"

"You're wonderful. And I think you for being so—so honest and open with me. But—"

"There is no 'but.' I am honest with you, *cara*, because of your honesty with me. I have learned to believe no one. People say what they think I want to hear, from the guy who wants to sell me a car to the CEO who wants to sell me his company. And women…" He shook his head. "They say, 'Yes, Marco,' and 'That's marvelous, Marco,' and they say it no matter what I do or say because they want to impress me." He cupped her face, threaded his hands into her hair. "You treat me as if I were a real man, sweetheart. You are who you are, no subterfuge, no lies, no games, and you expect the same of me. Do you have any idea how rare that is in my world?"

"Sometimes—sometimes people have reasons to be—to be less than honest."

"You have a kind heart. It is why you look for the best in others."

"There's good in everybody, Marco."

"You are the eternal optimist, Emily. I am a realist."

"A realist would understand that nobody is perfect."

He smiled. "You are such a beautiful innocent, *cara.*"

Sudden anger swept through her. How could an otherwise intelligent man make such an easy assessment of her? Did he still see her as a rain-soaked waif?

She put her hands on his chest and pulled back.

"Dammit, do not talk to me as if I were a child!"

Marco took her in his arms. She stayed motionless within his embrace. He murmured her name, kissed her temple, her chin, her mouth and, gradually, she let herself lean into him.

Staying angry at him was impossible, especially when she knew that her anger was really at herself and the fact that he saw her as someone she wasn't.

If she were known to him as Emily Wilde, raised in luxury, instead of Emily Madison, the rain-soaked waif he'd saved, would he still want her?.

She gave a long sigh and dropped her head to his shoulder.

"The world isn't all black and white," she said.

"*You* are my world, *Emilia mia.*"

He kissed her again and she forgot everything but him.

****

He took her shopping on l'Avenue Montaigne and l'Avenue George V.

Chanel. Vuitton. Prada. Givenchy. A dozen other places she'd never have thought of entering on her own.

Even the daughter of a general knew there were limits.

Marco didn't think so.

When she said that the pricing was so discreet there was no way to know what anything cost, he said she didn't have to worry about cost.

"The clothing allowance, remember?"

Yes, but how much was that allowance for? She told him that knowing the amount he'd budgeted was logical and necessary.

"I will tell you when we come close to going over it."

That would have made sense, but he couldn't see the prices, either, and she never once heard him ask.

He told her to let him worry about it.

He said it with such careless dismissal that the words *arrogant* and *male chauvinist* danced on the tip of her tongue, but he looked like a kid in a toy store, pointing at this and at that, beaming each time she tried something on and came out to the private fitting room to show it to him, and when she realized how happy he was, she didn't have the heart.

Instead, once she was alone with the sales clerk, she told her what she'd take and what she would not take.

In store after store, the clerks—the associates—smiled politely and said *oui, madame, certainement.* They said it so easily that she should have known the answers had nothing to do with reality, and when they returned to their suite hours later, the second bedroom was almost hidden beneath stacks of gaily wrapped boxes and beribboned shopping bags.

Marco had bought everything, or close to everything and when she protested he gave her a look that was serious and businesslike and he reminded her, again, of the clothing allowance.

When she began to protest, he looked at his watch, said they were running behind and she'd better get moving or they'd be late for their appointment.

"I thought the French deal was all done," she said.

He shrugged. "It is. All but this one last detail." He looked at his watch again. "You have half an hour, *cara*."

Half an hour?

Emily stared after him.

The man was impossible. He'd given her forty-five minutes last night. Thirty tonight. How could she get ready in such a rush? And if he really thought she'd keep all those boxes full of outrageously expensive clothing…

She knew buying her all those things had pleased him.

And yes, the job included a clothing allowance.

Did mistresses get clothing allowances? Was she, after less than a week, his mistress? Did he think she was? Because that was never going to happen. Bad enough she was already a woman he thought he knew but didn't; she would certainly never be in a relationship based on sex and availability.

And lies.

Her own lies.

Emily took a long, shaky breath.

How could things have gotten so complicated so fast?

She kicked off her shoes. Went into the bathroom. Turned on the shower, peeled off her clothes, stepped into the shower stall…

The glass door swung open. She gasped, turned, and found Marco, arms folded, standing there.

His posture was serious. His expression was serious.

And he was seriously naked.

So what? She was annoyed at him. Did he think sex could solve every problem?

"Would you please close the shower door?" she said. "It's cool in here."

He stepped inside the stall and shut the door behind him.

"That's not what I meant. I'm trying to take a shower."

"So am I."

"You gave me thirty minutes."

"You're down to twenty five."

"There's a shower in the other bathroom."

"There is a shower there. I agree. But there is a problem with it."

"What problem? It works just fi—"

"The problem," he said softly, "is that I am not in it with you."

He stepped under the spray and gathered her in his arms. She wanted to be angry or at least irritated but how could she be either of those things when she was in his arms?

Maybe he was right.

Maybe she truly was naïve.

And maybe everything was going much, much too fast.

"You are upset."

"Yes."

"Because I bought you those things?"

"That's part of it."

"What is the rest of it, then?"

She looked up into his eyes.

"Things are—things are happening too quickly. "

"Life happens quickly, *cara*."

She felt another little rush of anger. "Don't answer me with platitudes, Marco. I mean what I said. I feel as if—as if I'm traveling at the speed of light."

Marco raised her face to his and kissed her.

"We have to talk," she said.

"We do talk."

He kissed her again. And again. She felt the questions, the anger draining away.

"You said we had to be out of here in thirty minutes..." She caught her breath. "Don't. If you do that—"

"What?" he said gruffly. "What will happen if I do that?"

Lost, she could only cling to him, the center of her universe.

"We'll be late," she whispered.

"The Frenchman is a Frenchman," he whispered back. "He will figure out the reason and be happy for us."

She sighed. "Have I ever told you that you're impossible?"

His smile was wonderfully wicked.

"Have I ever told you that there is no such thing as impossible?"

He kissed her. Lifted her in his arms. And proved that he was right.

Nothing was impossible, especially when the water was warm and the moment was perfect—and you let all your concerns and doubts slip away.

****

The evening appointment went well.

The next day, Marco took a call from a German banker. As luck would have it, he, too, was in Paris and he had some business to discuss.

They met him for lunch.

The banker was tall and handsome. He gave Emily his very best smile, kissed her hand and rattled off something in German.

Emily laughed and rattled something in return.

Marco hung back a little as they were shown to their table.

"You didn't mention that you spoke German," he said softly.

"Well, I don't. I mean, not very well. Just a few

words, really."

She spoke more than a few words. By the end of the meal, the banker had agreed to all Marco's terms for acquiring a property the bank owned and why wouldn't he, when the man's major interest was clearly Emily?

Ridiculous.

This was business. The banker would not let his interest in a woman get in the way of that.

The banker said something to Emily that made her smile. The banker didn't just smile, he grinned.

Enough, Marco thought. He reached for her hand, threaded their fingers together and kept their joined hands on top of the linen-covered table.

Emily was startled. She was with him as his assistant, just as she had been last night.

Her eyes flashed a question. *What are you doing?*

His flashed an answer. *I am claiming you as exclusively mine.*

It was not very professional… but it made her heart soar.

The German looked from Emily to Marco. Then he gave a dramatic sigh.

"I am too late," he said ruefully.

"Much too late," Marco said, and brought Emily's hand to his lips.

****

She confronted him that night.

They were sitting on the terrace, drinking brandy.

She thought of a dozen ways to say it. In the end, what had been in her head for days was what she told him.

"I'm not Jessalyn," she said.

He looked at her as if she'd lost her mind.

"Why would you tell me that?"

"Because—because I won't be your mistress."

His eyes narrowed. "Have I asked you to be my mistress?" he said, his voice cold, his words clipped. And why did those words hurt?

"Good," she said. "Because I won't be. Not ever. I don't believe in that whole thing. You need to know that before—"

"I have no wish for you to be my mistress."

Stupid. The words did more than hurt. They twisted into her heart. She put down her brandy snifter; it tilted and amber liquid spread over the table. To hell with this, she thought, and shot to her feet.

"I'm tired, Marco. Good night."

"Emily."

He was on his feet, too.

She shook her head, started inside…

"Dammit, Emily," he said gruffly. He caught her arm, swung her toward him. "I have no wish for you to be my mistress." His expression softened; what she saw in his eyes made her breathless. "I want you to be my lover, as I am yours."

Tears rose in her eyes.

He saw them, drew her close, kissed them away.

"Something is happening between us," he said softly. "If you want the truth, it scares the hell out of me. But I am not going to walk away from it, *Emilia mia*, and I plead with you not to walk away from it either."

She began to weep.

Good tears, the kind that came from a heart full of joy.

Marco wrapped his arms more tightly around her.

"I am yours, Emily Madison. And you are mine."

She was. But she wasn't. She had to tell him that. Surely, it wouldn't matter. Not now that he knew her. The real her. Because everything that made her Emily Madison also made her Emily Wilde.

She hadn't set out to deceive him…

"Emily," he whispered, and she lifted her head from

his shoulder and kissed him, and once again, she let the world spin away.

****

They ended up staying an extra four days in Paris.

"But don't you have things on your calendar?" Emily said.

Marco shrugged. "As it turns out, I have an easy week ahead."

He didn't. He found himself wondering if that qualified as lying after that foolish, impassioned speech he'd made about lies and liars. No, of course it wasn't. A lie was something that caused hurt.

Telling Emily they could be here another few days, making the surreptitious phone calls necessary to cancel his appointments, was hurtful to no one.

Besides, that didn't matter.

This was Paris. It was a city of lovers.

There were so many wonderful things to see and do. They strolled through the Louvre. The Jeu de Paume. They walked the winding streets of Montmartre. They people-watched over *demitasse* at a sidewalk café on the Champs-Elysées. They went to Les Puces, the famous flea market that Emily had not been able to see when she and her sisters had been here visiting their father, because he hadn't approved.

She dropped that piece of information—that she and her sisters had been in Paris visiting their father—unexpectedly, and instantly regretted it. A flea market wasn't where she wanted to tell her lover the truth about herself, which she was increasingly desperate to do.

"So," Marco said as they held hands, walking down the long, crowded aisles of the market, "you have sisters?"

She nodded. "Uh-huh."

"How many?"

"Two."

"A nice-size family."

She looked at him. Should she tell him it was a bigger family than that? That she also had three brothers?'

Yes. She should.

"We're a big family," she said. "I also have three brothers. Half-brothers. Our father's first wife died and he married our mother."

"And everybody got along?"

"Yes. " She smiled. "We never think of each other as half anythings."

He laughed. "Did your father take your brothers to France, too?"

"Well, there's an age gap. Our brothers were away at school. We were still home."

"Ah. Must have been fun, a holiday like that."

She knew he was trying to reconcile what he thought, that she'd grown up poor, with a family that could afford a holiday in Europe.

"It wasn't actually a holiday. As I told Mrs. Barnett, my father was—is—in the army. We visited him when we could."

"It must have been difficult. Your mother, raising three girls and three boys with him gone."

"Actually, she died when we were little."

Marco let go of her hand, put his arm around her shoulders and drew her to his side. "And who took care of you?"

Nannies. The housekeeper. The ranch hands. And Jacob, Caleb and Travis when they weren't away at school.

"Hey."

She looked at Marco. He smiled, hugged her closer and kissed the top of her head.

"If it hurts too much to talk about—"

"No. It doesn't hurt. It's just, you know, it's kind of

complicated. There were—there were always lots of people around."

"Good. Grandparents. Aunts. Uncles. You were not alone, *cara*. I am happy to know that you were cared for and loved."

That much, at least, was true. She had been cared for and loved, though not by aunts and uncles and grandparents.

Her belly knotted.

She had to end this litany of omissions and half-truths. What had begun as a self-protective way of keeping people from seeing her as a Poor Little Rich Girl had turned into the kind of falsehood she would never have told this man she had come to care for.

Her throat constricted.

To care for? What a lifeless way to describe what she felt.

She loved him. With all her heart. With everything she was.

All the more reason to tell him the truth, but when she did…

Would he be upset? She sensed that he might be. But if he really cared for her…

He must.

She'd seen how he looked at her. When they were alone. When they were spending a simple day together. Or over dinner in the elegant restaurants where he was greeted like visiting royalty? The tiny bistros where the owners fussed over them?

"They hope we're from the Guide Michelin," she whispered to him that evening and Marco laughed and said she was probably right.

Or was she?

Watching her face that night, feeling the lightness in his heart, he suddenly wondered whether all the attention they were getting had less to do with the hope of being listed in a famous guidebook and more to do with a

French passion for discovering a man and a woman in love.

The thought would not go away.

Late that night, when sleep would not come, Marco pressed a light kiss to Emily's hair. Carefully, he took his arm from beneath her shoulders, pulled on his trousers, went out on the terrace and quietly closed the doors behind him.

Paris glittered with her own brilliant light, all but eclipsing the brightness of the moon and the stars.

He and Emily were lovers. But love?

The French were such romantics.

He was not.

He didn't believe in the concept. He had, once, but he'd been young. He'd thought that the grandmother and grandfather who'd taken him in would love him and when that had turned out to be nothing but a bitter hope, he'd believed that love would come with the nuns who'd replaced them.

What came, instead, were beatings and constant reminders that he had been born to a girl who had sinned.

By the time he came to America, he should have been past such nonsense. He wasn't. Fool that he was, he'd opted for one more attempt at love. His marriage. The woman who had claimed to love him, who had lied to him…

"Marco?"

That was what love was. Lies. Illusions. Delusions.

"Marco. Are you all right?"

He turned around.

Emily stood in the open doorway, his discarded white shirt hanging to her knees. Her hair was loose and wild, ivory radiance caught in among the long gold waves.

"I am—" He swallowed. "I am fine, c*ara.* I didn't mean to wake you."

"I woke because you weren't there."

Something happened to his heart.

He held out his arms. She went into them. And as he gathered her close and buried his face in her hair, he knew that he was a liar, too.

Love was real.

It was true.

Once you found the right person… As he had done.

The unbelievable had happened.

He was deeply, completely in love.

# CHAPTER TWELVE

The flight home went quickly.

Marco had a backlog of messages on his cell phone. He'd read through them in Paris and decided they could all be safely set aside, but by the time his plane was halfway over the Atlantic, he knew he had to get up to speed.

*"Cara,"* he said softly, "you must forgive me for a little while. I must deal with business."

Emily assured him that she understood.

Moments later, he was deep in calls on his satellite phone. When he reached for a stack of sticky notes and a pencil, she got to them first.

"Speakerphone," she mouthed.

He hit the switch. The man on the phone was still talking. Emily listened carefully and took notes. Marco covered the phone.

"You don't have to do this," he said quietly. "We're not at the office."

Her eyebrows rose. She grabbed a fresh sticky note and printed something on it. Then, with great drama, she slapped it on her silk jacket, jabbed her index finger at him, her thumb at herself.

Marco read the hand-printed sign and snorted with laughter.

*You employer,* it said. *Me employee.*

"Something the matter?" the guy on the other end of the phone asked.

Marco leaned over, took Emily's lips in a long kiss.

"Not a thing," he said, when he lifted his head. "Just my assistant reminding me that she's here to serve."

Emily stuck out her tongue. Marco winked, and then they settled into their roles.

That was the way it went each day at the office.

Marco was the boss. Emily was his PA His AA. She was, he said, the best thing that had happened to MS Enterprises in years.

She was also the best thing that had happened to its CEO.

They were inseparable.

They worked together during the day, attended business functions together in the evenings when they had to though the best evenings were the ones they spent alone, perhaps having dinner either at little West Village restaurants or at the elegant ones where only a man like Marco Santini could stroll in and get a table.

More and more, they ate in.

Steaks broiled in one of the fieldstone fireplaces. Chicken done on the terrace grill, which was finally getting a workout. Pasta from an Italian takeout on Lexington Avenue. Chinese from a wonderful hole-in-the-wall mom-and-pop all the way downtown near Mott Street. And, to his surprise and delight, Emily liked to cook. It turned out he did, too, under her laughing supervision.

On the weekends, they went down to the Union Square Greenmarket, bought bunches of this and bags of that. Then they went home and made dinner together.

He loved the weekends.

The weeknights? Not so much.

Sunday through Thursday, Emily insisted on going home at night, even if it was late.

"I can take a taxi," she'd say.

Marco wouldn't let her. He wouldn't wake Charles, either. Instead, he'd rise from their warm bed, pull on jeans and a shirt, grumble as he got the Ferrari from the new garage, grumble as he drove them to the East Village, grumble about the street, the building, her apartment and, especially, her bed.

It was too narrow, too short, too lumpy.

But he wouldn't leave her and even though she kept

telling him that was silly, she was glad he stayed because falling asleep without his arms around her was becoming impossible.

He said solving impossible problems was his field of expertise. They could solve this one if she moved in.

Her heart said, “do it.”

Her head said “not yet.”

It was too soon. Too much of a commitment. And there was still that thing about his not knowing that she wasn’t who or what he thought she was. There never seemed to be a good time to tell him.

So, she refused.

But she would stay on weekends.

Which was why the weekends were wonderful.

They walked the charming old streets of Soho, explored Central Park. They went to the Bronx Zoo and ate cotton candy and hot dogs; they went to the movies and he tried not to roll his eyes as she sobbed through a chick flick, but he knew better than to call it that.

Then Sunday would come and they were back to two residences even though her toothbrush was in his bathroom and lots of her clothes were in his dressing room.

It made Marco crazy.

As if that weren’t enough, she wouldn’t go to the office with him. Charles drove him. She took the subway. They did the same thing in reverse at the end of the day.

What would people think, she said, if they saw them coming to work, going from work, together?

That they were lovers, Marco thought, and cursed himself for ever having told her that business was business and pleasure was pleasure and the two didn’t mix. It turned out that they did mix. In was, in fact, a perfect combination

After several weeks, he decided to take things into his own hands.

He left his office. Charles was waiting. Normally,

they'd have driven home and Emily would arrive later. Taking the subway took much longer, especially at that hour.

But Marco, being Marco, had developed a plan.

Charles was an important part of it.

"Are you positive this will work?" he asked. Marco raised an eyebrow. Charles held his ground. "Are you positive this will work, *sir*?" he said.

Marco laughed. Then he sighed.

"No," he said. "But I am a desperate man."

And so, that evening, he got into the Mercedes. But instead of heading uptown, Charles drove to where Emily would board the subway. There were no parking spaces, of course, so he pulled up at a fire hydrant.

A few minutes later, they saw Emily hurrying along the opposite side of the street.

"You know what to do," Marco said.

Charles nodded. Marco got out of the car and ducked traffic as he ran across the street. He caught up to Emily as she was going down the steps to the subway station.

She glanced at him. Then she did the first double take he'd ever seen except in a movie.

"What are you doing here?"

"Experiencing the joys of rush-hour public transportation with you," he said cheerfully as he stepped on a discarded wad of chewing gum.

"I'm going downtown to my apartment to pick up a few things."

"An even longer ride. I am delighted."

"What's the matter with you, Marco?"

They reached the turnstiles. Emily had a transit card. Marco had come prepared and had one, too.

"Why should something be wrong with me?"

"I don't know but something is." She frowned at him. ""You're being foolish."

"I am not the one being foolish, *cara*."

The train was jammed. They hung onto straps side

by side. The woman to his left stood on his foot the entire trip; the guy behind him breathed garlic over his shoulder.

When they reached Emily's stop, Marco checked his watch. He had not expected Emily to go to her place. Not enough time had gone by for Charles to complete his errand.

"I am hungry," he said.

"I can make you something," she said. "Or we can send out—"

He took her hand.

"I am hungry now," he growled.

She raised her eyebrows. "Fine."

He marched her into a Thai restaurant. They'd made the mistake of eating there before. The food was either spicy enough to cause cardiac arrest or so bland it tasted like porridge. The wait staff should have been called the wait-forever staff; they were pleasant but that was how long it seemed to take for them bring menus, take orders and deliver food.

Emily thought of reminding him of those problems but one glance at his face and she changed her mind.

He seemed nervous.

Marco Santini, nervous?

Now she was nervous, too.

After they were finally served, they picked at their pad Thai and red curry. An hour dragged by. Marco looked at his watch. He turned in his seat, caught their waiter's eye.

"The bill," he barked.

"Whatever's wrong with you," Emily hissed, "don't let it out on him!"

He glared at her but he took a fifty from his wallet and added it to the money he'd already left. Then he marched her outside.

Charles and the Mercedes were waiting at the curb.

"What's Charles doing here?"

"He is here to take us home."

"I told you, I have to go to my place first."

Marco grabbed her hand and started walking her toward the limo.

"No, you do not."

"Yes, I do. I need—"

"You need nothing," he said, as Charles opened the rear door. "Is it done?"

"It is, sir."

"Is what done?" Emily said as she got into the car. "Really, Marco—"

"You are all moved in."

She blinked. "What is all moved in?"

Marco folded his arms as the car pulled into traffic. She knew what that meant. He'd reached some intractable position on some impossible subject. There were times he was worse than arrogant!

"Your things. Your clothes. Makeup. Books, jewelry, even your hair dryer. All of it is at my place. Right, Charles? "

"Right, sir."

Emily looked at the chauffeur in the mirror. His mouth curved in a very small smile.

"Let me get this straight," she said slowly. "You moved everything I own—*everything*—out of my apartment and into yours?"

Marco shrugged. "I suppose it is possible some small thing was overlooked. We will come down on the weekend and you can—"

She hit him.

Not hard.

It was more a punch to his shoulder and it made him want to laugh but he was not a foolish man and laughter, he was sure, would be a mistake.

"Do you remember my calling you arrogant? Well, you're not. You're—you're smug and self-centered and you will move all the stuff you took straight back because—"

"Emily. We need to change things. I want you with me, not in that unsafe hovel."

"It's not unsafe. It's not even a hovel. There are worse places."

"*Si.* The neighborhood where you worked."

"All cities have slums. Back in Dallas—"

"That's the point, sweetheart. I don't want you living as you did growing up. I want you to have all the things I can give you."

There it was again. The lie she lived with. The lie she could no longer live with.

"Marco. You have the wrong idea about how I grew up. I never said we were poor—"

"You don't have to explain."

"But I do! I didn't grow up poor. I grew up—"

"In a big family."

"Well, yes. "

"With a father who supported you on army pay." Marco took her hand. "I have money, *Emilia mia*. I am a wealthy man, and what is the point of all that wealth if I can't spend it on you?"

"I know what you think. How it looks. My apartment. The job playing piano." Emily swallowed hard. "See, I didn't have to live that way. I chose to. I wanted to be independent. I never had been, not in my whole life. My family—"

"Emily."

"Please. Please listen!"

"Sweetheart. I love you."

"You have the wrong idea about me," she said desperately, "and—and—" Her eyes widened. "What?"

Marco leaned forward, pressed the button that put the privacy screen in place. "I love you," he said. "I want us to live together. Do you understand? I love you. And you love me." He paused. For the first time since they'd met, she saw uncertainty in his face. "You do, don't you, *cara*? Because if you don't—"

Emily flung herself into her lover's arms.

****

A single rule remained.

It was the one about people seeing them together outside the formal setting of the office. And, Marco insisted, it was inane.

"We are together here the entire day. We go on business trips together. What can it possibly matter if we arrive at work and leave together?"

"It was your idea. Not to mix business with—"

"It was a foolish idea."

"If people see us coming in together and going home together, they'll suspect that we're… involved."

He laughed because they were, at that moment, very involved. They were in bed, she with her head on his shoulder, his arm tight around her, her thigh over his.

"Don't laugh at me," she said with mock indignation.

The truth was, he doubted they were fooling anybody. He knew damned well he couldn't keep his eyes off her, and each time she looked up and saw him watching her, she blushed in a way that made his hormones go crazy.

Not that any of that affected her competence.

She was the best assistant a man could ever hope to have. He didn't even think of her as his assistant anymore. She was his partner.

She composed most of his letters without needing any input from him. She wrote his reports and memos. She was his sounding board when he needed one; she was his first-line contact with his various department heads, all of whom seemed to think she was remarkable. She was his Keeper of the Door. Nobody got past her unless she knew that was what he wanted.

Not mixing business with pleasure had, until now, seemed logical. He'd always assumed having sex with a woman who worked for him would undermine office efficiency, but after six weeks, he knew that was patently untrue.

And they weren't having sex. They were making love. They were *in* love. Why shouldn't the world know it?

The realization hit him at work one afternoon in early November.

The world *would* know it if they took the next step. A logical step. One people took after they fell in love.

He fell into his chair. He wasn't ready for that. Not yet. No. Not yet.

Marco grabbed a handful of letters from his desk and buried his nose in them.

He read until he thought his eyes might glaze over.

One letter was particularly awful

It was a pompously-worded missive from a pompous bank that wanted him to build it a new world headquarters that would "enhance its image of tradition and privacy." And pomposity, he was thinking when he suddenly looked up, glanced out the open door of his office, saw Emily standing at the printer, frowning at it, her hands inky, her hair coming undone from the very demure pony tail she insisted on keeping it in for work, and the truth hit him, full force.

He was ready.

For that next step. For—a slight wave of panic roiled in his belly. For those things he'd never imagined even considering.

Marriage. Kids. A dog, a cat, a house in the country.

Crazy.

But that what love was all about. Being crazy. Crazy in love.

Marco put the letter down.

He wanted to marry Emily. The question was, would

she marry him?

She loved him, but in today's world, love didn't necessarily lead to marriage. Well, it had to, in his world. Maybe it was old-fashioned but in some ways *he* was old-fashioned.

What he needed was another plan.

Big steps required big plans. Part A and Part B, the first to take care of the nonsense about not letting people know about them, and the second…

The second involved a stop at Tiffany's.

*Dio!*

He took a deep breath. Exhaled. Took another. Exhaled again. Then he reached for the intercom and called Emily.

"I'm going to stay a little late tonight. Tidy up some loose ends."

"Sure. Just tell me what files we'll need and—"

"No, you go on. I'll tell Charles to meet you at the usual place. I'll grab a taxi later."

Silence. He almost smiled. He had confused her. That had been his intention. He'd just done away with what had become their new going-to-and-returning-from work arrangement, now that they were living together. Each morning, they rode together in the Mercedes, but Charles dropped her off a couple of blocks from the office. They picked her up at the same place each evening.

At least she wasn't experiencing the joys of the subway system anymore.

Now, tonight, Marco was telling her that he was sending her home alone.

"Are you sure?" she asked. "Because I don't mind staying."

"Positive. Is that OK?"

"OK," she said, and, rat that he was, it pleased the hell out of him that she sounded not just confused but unhappy at the prospect of not being with him.

Promptly at 6 p.m. she knocked politely at his door, then opened it. He looked up from the papers he was pretending to read.

"I'm leaving now."

He nodded, waved his hand. The distracted CEO at his best.

"Fine."

She didn't move. He knew she had to be waiting for him to get up, come over and kiss her. Instead, he kept his eyes on the papers. After a few seconds, the door closed.

Marco looked up. Plan A was underway.

He counted to ten. Then he shot from his chair, grabbed his suit jacket, stepped into the hall and checked to make sure Emily was not in sight. His heart was pounding. What if she wasn't ready for Plan A? Even worse, what if she didn't like Plan B?

Stop thinking, he told himself. Just run.

The receptionist looked up as he skidded past her desk.

"Mr. Santini? Is there something I can—"

Marco pulled open the heavy glass doors. *Dio,* his timing was off! The elevator was directly ahead and the doors were staring to shut.

He flew. Stabbed the call button. Jammed his hand between the doors.

They opened.

Emily looked at him and blinked.

"Marco?"

"Emily," he said, and he stepped into the car and took her in his arms.

"Marco! What are you—"

"Kissing you goodbye," he said. "And kissing you hello. And do not tell me about mixing business with pleasure, *cara*, unless you have forgotten that I make the rules here."

She raised her face to his. For one awful instant, he

couldn't read her eyes. Then she laughed and he laughed and he gathered her close and kissed her.

He heard the receptionist, who had a clear view of things from her desk, gasp. He heard the doors swish shut. He heard them open again on the lobby level, which would be crowded with his employees at this time of day.

It was just the audience he wanted, and he took all the time that kissing Emily deserved.

"You are mine," he said when, at last, he raised his head.

The look on her face turned his knees weak.

"Of course I am," she whispered, and he lifted her off her feet and swung her in a circle while she threw her head back and laughed.

****

He considered taking her with him to Tiffany's. Letting a woman pick out her own engagement ring was probably the modern way to do things, but there was nothing modern about falling in love.

So he told Charles to drive them home and he told her a small lie.

"I have to make a stop," he said, as she sat curled against him in the back of the Mercedes. "I promised a guy I'd meet him for a quick drink and the only way I'm going to get through it is to think of you on the terrace, wearing something that's going to make my blood pressure soar."

"It's too cool for the terrace," she said, running her index finger over his bottom lip. "I won't have any choice but to wait for you in bed."

The privacy screen was up. That meant he could slip his hand under the very businesslike skirt of her very businesslike suit. Beneath it, she wore very unbusinesslike thigh-high hose and an even more unbusinesslike silk thong.

The Mercedes pulled to the curb. She caught her breath as he skimmed his fingers under the thong.

"Don't be gone too long," she whispered.

"I won't, I promise."

"Because—"

"Because you'll miss me?"

She smiled. "I will. But—" Her smile tilted. "But we have to talk. About—about me. And my family. I haven't told them about us. About you. I haven't told you about them. And there's so much to tell you—"

"Your great-great-grandfather was a horse thief."

His tone was solemn but his eyes were filled with laughter. How could she not laugh, too?

"No?"

"No. But there are things—"

"Sweetheart." He leaned his forehead against hers. "What do I care if the Texas Madisons are not perfect?"

Emily flinched. "See? Even calling them that—"

"Not good?" He grinned. "Don't worry. I promise to mind my manners. I will speak properly to… I don't even know their names."

"My brothers are Jacob, Caleb and Travis. My sisters are Lissa and Jaimie. And—" she swallowed. "And my father—"

"I will salute your father," he said, trying to chase the serious expression from her face. "Shake hands with your brothers. Kiss your sisters." There was no answering smile. Was she worried about how he would deal with her family? Had she forgotten that he had not always lived in penthouses and ridden around in Ferraris and limousines? "Emily. Stop worrying. Everything will be fine."

"They won't be what you expect."

"They will be if they're like you."

Emily swallowed hard.

Why had she put off this moment? It wasn't as if she'd really lied. Lying by omission wasn't a lie…

Was it?

Besides, the truth wasn't so awful. So what if her brothers were rich, not just average working guys? If her father was a four-star general? If she'd been raised in luxury in what was, in effect, a private kingdom?

So what if he believed she was the one person in his life who'd always told him the truth?

Her heart lodged in her throat.

"Marco," she said quickly. "Cancel your meeting. Can you do that? Come upstairs with me instead and—"

His cell phone beeped. A text message. He pulled it from his pocket and read it.

Hell.

Tonight, of all nights, when he wanted to be alone with his Emilia…

"What's the matter?"

He looked up. "Nothing. Just a text from an old pal. He's in New York with his wife. An unexpected layover. Mechanical troubles with their plane. He thought it would be nice if we got together for dinner."

Emily nodded. "Of course," she said softly. "You go ahead. Take the meeting you had planned and then meet up with your friend. I'll—I'll catch up on some reading."

"I have a better idea. I'll run my, ah, my errand. And I'll phone my friend and tell him and his wife to come to my place—to our place, *cara.* I want you to meet them. We'll have drinks and then we can go out for dinner or order in. How does that sound?"

It sounded like yet another night when the truth would have to wait. Still, it had waited this long…

"Sweetheart? You'll like them, I promise."

"I'm sure I will." She forced a quick smile. "It sounds like fun."

"*Si.* It will be." He cupped her cheek as Charles pulled the Mercedes to the curb in front of the condo. "I won't be long."

The doorman opened the rear door. Emily stepped

on to the sidewalk. Marco leaned up. She leaned down. They shared a soft kiss.

He waited until she'd gone through the door and into the lobby. Then he put down the privacy screen.

"Charles? We are going to Tiffany's."

Charles looked in the mirror and smiled.

"Congratulations, sir."

"Is it that obvious?"

"It's been that obvious for a while," Charles said.

Yes, Marco thought as the limo pulled away from the curb, it definitely had.

Why had it taken him so long to see it?

Traffic was heavy. He had lots of time to plan what would happen tonight once he and Emily were alone. He'd have the ring he was about to buy in his pocket. He'd take her out on the terrace—it was cool but he wanted the stars and the city lights to add their own magic. Then he'd get down on one knee and ask her to be his wife.

They were almost at Tiffany's. Marco took out his phone and hit a speed dial button.

"Hello?" a slightly-accented male voice said.

"Khan, you desert reprobate, what are you doing on my turf?"

His Royal Highness Sheikh Khan ibn Zain al Hassad, Reigning Prince of Altara, laughed.

"It's good to hear your voice, Marco. How are you?"

"I'm fine. Actually, I'm great. And you?"

"I am happier than I have ever been," Khan replied. "Marriage agrees with me."

"I'm sorry I missed your wedding."

"I am, too, but I understood. You were in South America, as I recall."

"Yes. Brazil. So, how is your bride?"

"Laurel is pregnant," Khan said, his voice rich with pride. "And here's your chance finally to meet her."

"I'm looking forward to it. How about coming for

drinks and dinner? You know my address. Say, about eight?"

"We don't want you to put you to any trouble."

"It won't be any trouble; it'll be a pleasure to see you again and to meet Laurel." Marco cleared his throat. "There will, ah, there will be someone with me."

"Truly, we don't want to inconvenience you. If you have a date tonight—"

"She's not my date. She is—" What? Emily was no longer his lover. She was the woman he was going to marry, but how could he say that to his friend when he had not said it to her? "I want you to meet her. Her name is Emily. Emily Madison. She's from Dallas."

"Well. Emily and Laurel will have something in common. Laurel's from there, too."

"Right. I remember that."

"For all we know, they might even have friends in common. You know that six-degrees-of-separation thing."

"Anything is possible."

"Well," Khan said, "we'll see you at seven."

He ended the call, turned to his wife and took her in his arms.

"We're going to Marco's place."

"Mmm," Laurel said. "That's nice."

Khan lowered his head and brushed his lips over hers.

"There's a new woman in his life."

"Something serious?"

"I don't think so. He's never serious about women. Besides, he sounded nervous mentioning her."

"Do you think we've come on the scene at a bad time?"

Khan sighed. "What I think," he said, "is that we're better off not speculating. All Marco said is that she's from Texas. From Dallas."

"Really? What's her name?"

“Emily. Emily Madison.”

“Nope, I don’t know her. The only Emily I know is Emily Wilde.”

Laurel rose on her toes and looped her arms around her husband’s neck.

“How much time do we have?”

“Just under two hours.” His eyes darkened. “Why? Did you have something you wanted to do first?”

She put her lips to his ear. Khan listened, gave a sexy growl and swung her into his arms.

“Impertinent female,” he said, and kissed her.

“Damned right,” she said, laughing as he carried her into their bedroom.

# CHAPTER THIRTEEN

Had the elevator to the penthouse always been so slow?

Emily tapped her foot impatiently as the mirrored car made its climb. She'd been so caught up in Marco's kissing her in front of all those people, then in all that talk about her family that she was already in the elevator before she realized the importance of what was happening tonight.

Marco had invited an old friend and his wife to join them for drinks and dinner.

Such a simple thing.

Except, it wasn't.

She'd met lots of his business acquaintances, but this was Marco's friend. His old friend. He was bringing his wife and they were coming here, to the home Marco and she shared.

The world, her life, everything was changing. She'd met a man, gone to work for him, fallen in love with him and now they were a couple.

So much had happened in only—what?—six weeks.

And nobody knew about any of it. She'd spoken with her sisters a few times, with her brothers, even with her father. They all led busy lives; keeping in touch by telephone had long ago become important. She'd spoken with Nola, too.

But not once had she mentioned Marco.

They all knew she had a new job at a company called MS Enterprises, but that was it. She hadn't said anything more.

Now, she wanted them to know all about him. The man she adored. She just had to tell him a few things about herself first, but she wasn't going to think about that now.

There was too much to do, getting ready for the first visit they'd had as a couple.

Well…not really. In fact, there was hardly anything to do.

Everything was shiny and spotless. Emily reached for a throw pillow on one of the white linen sofas, fluffed it and put it back. She straightened a lampshade. A cleaning service came in three times a week to dust and polish and clean. Marco's housekeeper came in those same three days to do the laundry, fill the fridge and freezer, cook meals and freeze them.

Travis called it living the bachelor life.

Damn. She wasn't going to think about Travis or her brothers tonight.

She plucked another pillow from the sofa and punched it into shape. She had to get all that stuff about her family out of her head. Think about tonight. What snacks to serve with drinks.

Better still, what to wear.

Dinner wasn't a problem.

Marco had said they'd go out or perhaps order in. Either way would be fine. He could always get an excellent table at any of the best restaurants in the city, even when he didn't have reservations, and those restaurants would gladly deliver to their door.

It was the same for her brothers.

Emily stood still, tossed the pillow on the sofa and took a deep breath. Slowly, deliberately, she let it out.

She was turning herself into a nervous wreck.

Meeting his friends was scary enough. Knowing that her charade was about to come to an end was worse.

What was she going to say? *Marco, I have something to tell you. My father isn't just a soldier; he's a general. And I'm not really from Dallas; I'm from a half-million-acre ranch called El Sueño. I grew up pampered and rich and I never stood on my own two feet until I got to New York.* Or maybe she should simply say

*Here's the thing, Marco. There is no Emily Madison.*

Her cell phone rang. Emily jumped at the sound, then dug for the device in the depths of her shoulder bag.

"Hello?"

"*Cara.*"

Edgy as she was, just hearing his voice made her smile. "Hi."

"I'm on my way home."

"Good. That's good. I'll be showered and dressed by the time you get here."

"Don't."

"Don't what?"

"Shower and dress." His voice was low and husky. "Wait for me."

"But your friends…"

"Wait for me," he said. "Just another few minutes."

She heard the sound of his phone disconnecting. Disconsolate, she stared at hers until the screen went dark.

She remembered all the times she, Jaimie and Lissa had talked about men. Agreeing that guys were a good thing to have around had been easy. For sex and heavy lifting, Jaimie or maybe Lissa had said, and they'd all laughed.

They'd never mentioned love.

The truth was, she hadn't thought about love. It had always been something way, way out there in the future, kind of like death and taxes and whether or not you'd ever use Botox.

And now here she was, not just in love but desperately in love. With the only man she would ever want, the only man she hoped to spend her life with. And everything he knew about her was untrue.

Wrong.

The details were untrue.

She wasn't.

She was the woman he'd fallen in love with. She

was Emily no matter what her last name was.

He would see that, understand it, accept it.

The sun dropped lower. The sky began to darken. And just when she knew she was going to weep, she heard the elevator give its soft sigh as it rose toward the penthouse.

She swung around. Never mind that guests were coming. Never mind anything but the truth. She would confess right now…

The doors opened.

Marco came out of the elevator with his suit coat off, his shirt unbuttoned, his eyes blazing with passion.

"*Amore mio,*" he said, and she went into his arms and forgot everything, everything but him.

****

Marco paced through the big living room, back and forth, back and forth, the ring he'd bought damn near burning a hole in his pocket.

It was perfect.

It was, wasn't it?

He had looked at enough rings to make his head spin, all of them beautiful, some of them spectacular, none of them The One. The saleswoman had done her best to help. What size stone did he want? What shape? What kind of setting? Logical questions but his only answer was that he'd know the right ring when he saw it.

And, finally, he had.

It was a flawless blue-white three-carat diamond set in platinum and flanked by cornflower-blue sapphires. Beautiful yet modest and with a fiery heart. Just like his Emilia.

He grinned as he took it from his pocket and looked at it.

OK. Maybe the ring wasn't so modest, but Emily was. And beautiful. And fiery.

He could hardly wait to slip the ring on her finger. He'd had to guess at the size but why worry about that when it suddenly hit him that what he really had to guess at was whether she would say "yes" to his proposal.

She loved him but the only certainty in this life was that Emily was the missing half of him.

He loved her in bed. He loved her out of bed. She was smart, she was fun, he could discuss absolutely anything with her, and she wasn't afraid of standing up to him.

And he trusted her. With everything he was or ever would be. His soul. His life. His heart.

*Dio,* he was a wreck.

If only Emily would appear—but she had all but thrown him out of their bedroom.

"I can't get dressed with you watching me," she'd said.

"Why?"

"Because I want to look perfect, that's why!"

He'd smiled, stepped behind her at the cheval mirror, cupped her shoulders and kissed the side of her throat.

"You already do."

"You don't understand. I'm meeting your friends."

"And?"

She'd sighed the kind of long-suffering sigh he knew women gave when men were too thick-headed to understand the mysteries women were born understanding.

"And, I'm nervous."

"*Cara*. They are nice people."

"I'm sure they are but—but I'm just on edge. So please, wait for me downstairs."

Well, he had waited. And waited. First in the living room. Now on the terrace. Maybe the cool night air would calm him. Maybe he'd stop second-guessing himself. Had he chosen the right ring? Should he have taken Emily with him? What if she said, *It's a pretty ring and it's very nice of you to ask me but—*

"Marco?"

Emily's voice was soft. He put the ring in his pocket, turned around—and almost stopped breathing.

She was wearing red. Red silk, red chiffon—he'd never been very good at telling one kind of fabric from another. He only knew that the dress was incredible. It had thin straps and it skimmed her body while somehow clinging to all the right places. Her shoes were black strappy things with nosebleed heels. Her hair was loose, the way he loved it; she was wearing long pearl earrings that he'd bought for her at a tiny shop in Soho just last week.

"Art nouveau," the vendor had assured them.

Marco had known only that they looked as if they'd been made for the woman he loved.

She flashed a quick, nervous smile. "I didn't overdo? I mean the dress…"

He held out his arms and she went straight into them. *"Tu sei bella, cara mia."*

Her smile warmed. *"Grazie, signor. Anche tu bello."*

Marco framed her face with his hands. His heart was so full. To hell with waiting until later. He would give her the ring now, ask to her be his forever…

Beep.

"*Emilia,"* he said, "*il mio cuore ..."*

Beep.

"Sweetheart." Emily put her hand over his. "It's the intercom."

The intercom. He had been about to propose. Besides that, the woman he loved had just called him "sweetheart." No woman had ever called him that before.

"To hell with the intercom."

"It's probably the concierge saying that your friends are here. Remember?"

His friends. Khan and Laurel. Talk about bad timing…

He took her hand, kissed it, then tucked her arm within his. Together, they walked through the living room to the foyer, where he plucked the white house phone from the wall.

"Mr. Santini. Your guests are here, sir."

"*Si*. Excellent. Please send them up."

He put his arm around Emily's waist. She looked up at him.

"You sure I look all right?" she whispered, as if her words might carry into the rising elevator car.

He tilted her face to his and gave her a slow, tender kiss.

*"Molto bella."*

Emily smiled. The light above the elevator blinked as the car came to a gentle stop.

Marco gave her one last kiss just as the doors slid open...

Laurel gasped. "Emily?"

Khan shook his head. "I don't understand. Marco? You never said… Emily? Emily Wilde?"

And the world came apart.

****

Scant moments later, Marco and Emily were alone, he tight-lipped with cold fury, she weeping in despair.

She sat in the middle of one of the sofas, a pillow she'd fluffed to within an inch of its life not an hour ago clutched to her breasts like a life preserver.

Marco was pacing the same path he'd paced earlier tonight as a nervous suitor but now his footsteps were heavy, his hands were fisted in his trouser pockets, and the look on his face said that nothing in the world would ever be the same again.

"I tried to tell you," she said in a trembling voice. "I

tried and tried but you wouldn't listen."

"You told me nothing," Marco snarled. "Not one damned thing!"

"I did. I said you had the wrong idea about me, that I—that I wasn't the small- town girl you'd decided I was."

"I decided? I decided nothing except to believe your sad story."

"I didn't tell you a sad story. You're the one who—"

"Did you tell me you worked as a piano player in a bar?"

"Yes. And it was the truth."

"Did you tell me that you lived in that—that abominable slum?"

"I *did* live there. And it wasn't an abominable sl—"

"Perhaps it was I who I decided your father had spent his life being shuffled from army base to army base."

"You're distorting everything! I never said—"

"Or perhaps it was my decision to think of your brothers as—as men who went to work each morning and clocked in to their jobs!"

"I never said any such thing."

"You never said they were the Wildes of Wilde's Crossing, either."

Emily narrowed her eyes. "I see. So being the Wildes of Wilde's Crossing makes them better than if they worked with their hands?"

"I did not mean—"

"Because if that's your problem—"

"My problem," he said coldly, "is that I was allowed to think that your family could not help you lead a more comfortable life and yet one of your brothers is an investor with the power of an emperor, another is an attorney who is the first choice of corporate powerhouses everywhere and the third is a man who manages a ranch the size of a small nation and breeds horses that sell for more money than most people will earn in their lifetimes!"

Emily rose from the sofa, still clutching the pillow.

"I tried to tell you the truth. Several times. And, just for your information, I didn't want their help."

"That is not the point!"

"Then what is? Are you saying that my brothers are too successful? That would be a strange complaint from a man who owns an international conglomerate that makes millions upon millions of dollars each year."

Color suffused his face. She knew that wasn't what he'd meant, but anger was creeping in to replace despair. And she welcomed it.

"I am not saying that!"

"No?"

"No. I am saying that letting me believe the Madisons were an average American family was a falsehood. Hell, letting me believe they even existed was a lie!"

"What if it was? It didn't harm anyone."

"It created a woman who did not exist!"

"I changed my name," Emily said, "not who I am inside!"

"You let me think you were someone you are not."

Emily flung the pillow across the room. "Meaning what? That you got off on showing the world to a little country girl?"

His jaw tightened and she regretted the words as soon as she'd said them. The accusation was all wrong. He'd wanted to make her happy, that was all.

And he had.

"I didn't mean that," she said quickly. "I know that wasn't why you—"

"Perhaps it was. Perhaps that was all this was."

"No. I don't believe that."

He didn't answer. His expression was stony. Emily took a step forward.

"Marco." Her voice softened. "Don't you want to know why I became Emily Madison?" He folded his arms. God, she hated when he did that! "I couldn't get a job. I couldn't get anybody to see me as a real person."

His lips pulled back from his teeth in a thin parody of a smile.

"Perhaps that is because you are not a real person, Ms. Madison."

"Dammit, the name is rightfully mine. It's my middle name. It's right on my birth—"

"The more you say, the worse it becomes."

"What's that supposed to mean?"

"What does it say on your passport, hmm? Emily Madison? Or Emily Wilde?"

"Emily Wilde. But what—"

"Do you recall handing your passport to my co-pilot when we flew to Paris? He took it to airport security. Strangers read that passport and knew your name was Wilde even as I believed it was Madison!"

She gave a strangled laugh. "How does that even matter?"

How, indeed? Marco knew that she was right. What mattered was that this woman, whom he had believed to be so honest, so innocent, so pure of heart and mind that she was unlike anyone he'd ever known, had made a fool of him.

He, the man who had never needed anyone, had let himself need a woman who didn't exist.

He'd been had. Scammed. Made a laughing stock, although he sure as hell didn't feel like laughing.

Marco swung away and walked to the other end of the room. He dug his right hand into his trouser pocket, felt the ring he'd dropped inside it what seemed like an eternity ago. The ring he'd bought for Emily Madison, the woman he'd wanted to be with for the rest of his life.

He stopped, his back to her, and closed his eyes, saw once again the shocked look on Khan's face, the bewilderment on Laurel's.

He spun around.

"How could you have done this to me?"

"I didn't do anything to you." Emily's eyes filled with tears. "I love you. I never meant to hurt you."

"You deceived me."

"I keep telling you. I didn't mean to deceive you. I was caught in a web, don't you understand? And whenever I tried to tell you the truth, either you stopped me—or I lost courage."

"You lost courage," he said, his words flat and cold. "Charming. Did you think so little of me that you believed I would stop caring for you if I knew you were a woman named Emily Wilde and not a woman named Emily Madison?"

Emily gave a short, sharp laugh.

"Take a look at what's happening now and we'll see if you still want to ask me that question."

"That is a distortion of the facts. I only learned the truth because someone found you out." His face darkened. "That I should have had the blindfold torn from my eyes by strangers…"

"They aren't strangers. Khan is your friend. Laurel is mine."

"Exactly. Friends who now see how I was duped."

Emily swiped the tears from her eyes with the back of her hand. Anger was changing to fury. Given a choice, it was the better emotion.

"Is that what this is all about? Your ego?"

"It is about your lies."

"Give me a break. It's about you. It's always about you and your high and mighty arrogance."

"I am not arrogant," Marco said and even in his cold rage, he winced at the stupidity of what he'd said.

Emily strode toward him, chin up, eyes blazing. "In fact, arrogance is the one real emotion you possess."

"Arrogance is not an emotion. And do not try to

change the subject! The point is, you lied to me."

"The point is, I didn't lie to you. I was already lying when I met you…"

She broke off in mid-sentence, as stung by the truth of her admission as by the stoniness of his expression.

There was a second truth here, as well. A terrible truth.

"You fell in love with Emily Madison," she said softly.

"Such a brilliant revelation!"

"You fell for some—some symbol of perfection."

"I do not know where you are going with this."

"But I'm not perfect, Marco." She flung out her arms. "I am what you see. A woman. Flawed. Imperfect. You can't label me. I'm not any one thing. I'm many things and not all of them are good. The only certainty is that I love you."

"You love me."

"Yes. I love you."

Silence stretched between them. He looked at her. A pain so sharp it almost brought him to his knees knifed through him. He had bared his soul to this woman. He had given her his heart.

What mistakes to have made! To have forgotten the lessons of his childhood, his manhood, his marriage…

He was not good when it came to seeing through women's lies.

"Marco," Emily whispered. "I love you."

Her voice broke; she was weeping again. He felt a muscle knot in his jaw as she held out her hand.

*Take it,* a voice inside him implored. *Put aside your pride and take her hand.*

But he didn't. Instead, he heard himself say the words that would haunt him to the end of time.

"For all I know, that is just another lie."

Her head shot back, as if he'd hit her. He thought she was going to break down completely, but she didn't.

Instead, the shimmer of tears in her eyes became the glitter of ice.

"You're right," she said. "I don't love you. I pity you."

He watched her turn on her heel and walk away from him, her pace quickening, as she got closer to the foyer. Her handbag was on a glass table where she'd left it hours ago; she'd left a black pashmina there, as well, in case they had dinner out. Now, she grabbed the shawl, wrapped it around her shoulders and then picked up her purse. The only sign of what she might be feeling came when she reached the elevator and hit the call button with her fist.

The doors whisked open.

Marco felt his heart start to thud.

"Emily," he said…

Too late.

The doors shut.

And Emily was gone.

# CHAPTER FOURTEEN

Thanksgiving had always been Emily's favorite time of the year.

There was something about the idea of families gathering together that was warm and real.

When she was little, really little, she and Jaimie and Lissa would spend the day before Thanksgiving in the kitchen, helping their mother and the housekeeper, getting in the way, spilling flour and sugar and making cookie cutouts of their hands.

And, at night, it meant getting down the big picture book with Santa and his sleigh and reindeer on the cover.

Her mother had said that reading "'Twas the Night Before Christmas" starting on Thanksgiving Eve had always been a tradition when she was growing up. She said she had no idea why, but now it was a tradition she kept, too. So each year, the night before Thanksgiving, the sisters and, when they were young, Travis, Jacob and Caleb had all gathered around her and, together, they read the classic old poem with lots of *Ho-Ho-Ho's* and improvised ringing of reindeer bells and even the beat of tiny hooves.

Their father had been stationed half a world away. He'd phoned to wish them a happy holiday; Caleb, Travis and Jake were all home from school and they'd done their big-brotherly best to keep their little half-sisters happy, but at midnight Lissa had awakened and started to cry. Emily and Jaimie had climbed into her bed and they'd wept and wept until their brothers heard them, came into the bedroom and turned on the light.

They'd taken one look at the three sobbing little girls and asked no questions.

Jake had climbed onto Lissa's bed and gathered all three girls into his arms.

"'Twas the night before Christmas," he'd said without having to ask what they needed to hear and without the book, too, because they'd all heard the poem so often.

And while he told them the well-loved story, Caleb and Travis had gone downstairs, Travis to make cocoa, Caleb to pile a plate with cookies.

After a few years, it seemed silly to read a children's poem every night for almost a month. Besides, Emily, Jaimie and Lissa certainly didn't believe in Santa anymore. Their brothers were sometimes away, Caleb off doing what he solemnly called Secret Stuff in heaven only knew where, Travis and Jake flying jets and helicopters, and it was a given that the general would not be there but would send a card with a Pilgrim on the front or pay a Skyped visit.

This Thanksgiving, except for the general, the Wildes were together.

Emily, Lissa and Jaimie had all flown in, and Caleb was there with his Sage, Jacob with his Adoré, Travis with his Jennie. There were babies there, as well: Travis and Jennie's little girl, Eleanor; Caleb and Sage's little boy, Cameron; and, as Jake proudly announced, his hand curved protectively over his wife's slight belly bump, she was pregnant, not just with one baby but two—"By God, we're having twins!" he'd said.

There would be even more little Wildes on hand at the next gathering of the clan.

On Thanksgiving Day, Jaimie put together champagne cocktails for everyone but Adoré, who got a glorious concoction of club soda and freshly squeezed orange juice topped with a sprig of mint.

The housekeeper had the day off. Lissa cooked a feast. An enormous stuffed, roasted wild turkey took place of honor, but there was also a huge roast beef, asparagus, baked brussels sprouts, three kinds of potatoes, bread pudding, apple, mince and pumpkin pies.

Emily brought out the handmade chocolates she'd found in a beautiful little shop in Soho, tiny truffles and creams that, Jaimie said, put five pounds on your hips just to look at them.

Everyone drank, ate, laughed, played with the two littlest Wildes and talked about what they'd been doing since they'd last seen each other.

When it came to that topic, Emily was conspicuously silent. Well, her sisters agreed, she'd been kind of quiet altogether.

Maybe something was wrong.

Her sisters waylaid her in the kitchen.

"Em?" Lissa said. "What's the matter?"

"Nothing," she said brightly. "Why would anything be the matter? What kind of question is that?"

A very good question, Lissa and Jaimie thought, exchanging glances. Jaimie cleared her throat.

"Well, you haven't had much to say."

"Neither have you," Emily said.

Jaimie colored a little. Lissa looked at her. It was true. Jaimie had been pretty quiet, too.

"Work," Jaimie said briskly, waving her hand. "I'm all tied up with stuff. Things are stabilizing a little, people are putting their houses on the market…" She frowned. "And we weren't talking about me, we were talking about Emily."

"Emily is standing right here," Emily said, trying to sound amused. "Let's not talk about her as if she weren't."

"Well, no. Let's be more direct than that," Lissa said, opening one of the four big wall ovens and peering inside. "We're all talking about what's new in our lives. You haven't opened your mouth."

"If you're checking on those pies, I think the crust on the one in the top oven might be—"

"Don't you want to tell us about your new job?"

"What new job?" Emily said. "Lissa, really, that

pie—"

"The one you called and told me about," Jaimie said. "The personal assistant thing."

Emily swallowed hard.

"Oh. That."

"Yes. Oh. That. How's it going?"

Emily turned on the water in the sink, reached for the coffee pot.

"I quit."

"How come?"

"I just did. Hand me the canister, will you?"

"Yeah, but why? It sounded like a great job."

"Well, it wasn't. And I don't want to talk about it, OK? Just hand me the coffee."

Voices, laughter, the sounds of people greeting people flooded the house. Footsteps made their way down the hall. The Wilde sisters turned around…

And Emily went pale.

"Laurel?" she said. "What are you doing here?"

The women stared at each other. "Khan and I flew in for the holiday. Didn't Jake tell you? He invited us."

"Khan's here, too?"

"Of course he's here, too. Emily. Em. I'm so sorry about what happened that night. Neither of us ever dreamed—"

"What night?" Lissa said.

"What happened?" Jaimie said.

"Nothing happened," Emily said, and she looked up and saw her brothers crowded into the kitchen, Khan standing just in front of them, and the world tilted. "Not a goddamned thing happened," she said, and she dumped the coffee pot into the sink and fled.

****

The thing about having a big family was that you couldn't escape them.

The thing about running was that you couldn't escape what you were running from.

And the thing about spending the last ten days telling yourself that you hated the man who'd broken your heart was that it was a lie, and as she'd already so horribly proved, she wasn't a very good liar.

Jaimie knocked on her door. "Em? Come on out. We won't ask you any questions."

Lissa tried next. "Honey? Please come out. No questions, I swear."

Talk about lies…

Afternoon gave way to evening.

Her sisters tried again. They rattled the doorknob, said they were driving into town. Mr. Upton, the postmaster, had phoned. It was a holiday and the post office was closed but somehow or other, a bunch of packages had arrived anyway. From the general—he always sent Christmas gifts early—and, of course, Mr. Upton knew they had to be dealt with. The female contingent—Lissa, Jaimie, Adoré, Jennie, Laurel and Sage—were driving into town to pick them up. Why didn't she come with them?

She considered it. She was all cried out and she had to face everybody eventually. But she considered it for too long because the next thing she heard was the sound of an SUV driving away.

OK.

Her sisters were gone.

Her brothers were still here but they'd be easier to deal with. Men were uncomfortable with emotional stuff. She could silence them with a look.

Besides, what had happened to her was none of their business. She had no need to give in to badgering and questioning, assuming they tried any of that.

She rose from the bed where she'd thrown herself hours ago. Turned on the lights. Showered. Changed into jeans and a long-sleeved cashmere sweater. Brushed her hair, pulled it back in a ponytail and scrubbed her face. No makeup. She wasn't in the mood for makeup, wasn't in the mood for artifice of any kind.

One last deep breath and she opened the bedroom door and marched downstairs to face reality.

The Wilde brothers and Khan, a brother by attitude if not by birth, were all in the kitchen, seated around the enormous oak table that was older than any of them. No babies in sight. Evidently, they'd been put to bed.

There was a platter of huge man-ready sandwiches in the center of the table. Everybody had a big mug of something steaming hot, coffee or tea or maybe hot toddies.

All at once, on top of being in no mood for interrogation, she was also hungry and thirsty.

Emily straightened her shoulders and marched into the room.

Every head swiveled toward her.

"Em," Jake said.

"Honey," Travis said.

"Sis," Caleb said.

"Emily," Khan said, and cleared his throat.

She nodded, went to the stove, took down a mug and poured herself some coffee. Got a plate from the cupboard, a spoon, knife and fork from the silverware drawer. She liberated a while linen napkin from the shelf. Then she went to the empty space at the foot of the table, pulled out the chair and settled into it.

The men watched her.

She reached for the platter of sandwiches.

Four pairs of hands reached out to help her. She glared. The hands drew back. She leaned over the table. The sandwiches were halved; each half looked substantial enough to feed a family of four.

"I made them," Jake said proudly.

Emily nodded, took a half of what looked to be ham, cheese, turkey, beef and a couple of dozen other things and put it on her plate. She picked it up again, realized there was no way she could possibly get her mouth around it, put it down, took her knife and fork and sawed off a corner.

The men watched her.

She put the piece in her mouth. Chewed, even though the thing seemed unchewable. Swallowed. Took a sip of coffee. Sawed off another piece of sandwich.

The men went on watching her,

She swallowed. Drank a little coffee. Cleared her throat. If she talked about eating the sandwich with a knife and fork, maybe she could keep them from trying to talk about anything else.

So she tried what she hoped was a smile.

"I don't normally do things like this," she said, "but—"

"But you did."

She looked at Caleb. His voice was stern, that big-brother tone in it he'd occasionally used on all the sisters when they were in their teens.

"Well, yes. I know it doesn't look good. But what else could I do? I mean, all that size and heft..."

A fist hit the table. Emily swung her head toward Travis.

"Jesus H. Christ, we don't want to hear that kind of stuff!"

"Huh?"

"So, that was it? The guy turned you on so bad that you agreed to be his mistress?"

Emily blanched. "What the hell are you talking about, Jacob?"

Travis: "You know what! We're talking about your—your paramour."

Any other time, she would have laughed.

Caleb: "Your lover."

Jacob: "The guy who seduced you. Marco Santini, the son of a bitch!"

Emily stared at her brothers. She had never seen them so furious. The hard, handsome faces. The cold eyes. The tension visible in the set of their shoulders.

And Khan.

He looked exactly the same. Angry. Furious. Totally and completely pissed off.

She put down her knife and fork, wiped her mouth with her napkin.

"Listen to me," she said carefully. "Listen well, because I'm only going to say this once. This is none of your business!"

Jacob: "The hell it isn't!"

"It isn't. It's my business. Period."

Travis: "It's our business, kid, and don't you forget it."

"It is not your business," she said coldly, "and I am not a kid!"

"You're our baby sister."

"I am your twenty-four-years-old sister. Not your baby sister. Got it?"

"Why in hell didn't you come home?"

Emily swung toward Jake. "Oh, I don't know," she said coldly. "Why didn't you come home after you were discharged from the hospital?"

"I did."

"No. You did not. You dropped by, stayed for a while, then took off."

Jake shot to his feet. "That was different."

"How was it different?"

"I'm a guy. You're a girl. You're our sister."

Emily threw down her napkin and stood up. "That's such bull, Jacob!"

"It's not bull."

"It is," she said, turning toward Caleb. "Dammit, that's what I've been my entire life. One of the Wilde girls. The Wilde sisters. The youngest one, the one who needs to be protected from the real world."

"That's not true," Travis said.

Emily looked at Khan. "And you. Couldn't you keep quiet? Couldn't you keep what you saw to yourself?"

He rose slowly from his chair, his eyes dark, his mouth thinned.

"I did. For all this time. I kept quiet because Laurel said if you wanted help from us or your family, you'd ask."

Emily raised her chin. "Smart woman you married."

"But I could not keep quiet any longer." His eyes narrowed. "I liked Marco. I believed him to be a good man. I never imagined, *never* imagined, that he would take the sister of my friends as his mistress."

Emily snorted.

"Lovely. Mistresses are OK so long as they aren't the sisters of anybody you know."

Khan's face reddened. "You are twisting my words." He paused; she could tell he was trying to compose himself. "I would not have spoken, Emily. I would have kept my counsel… but when you ran, your family had questions. And they told me they were worried about you. That you have not been yourself. That you have been very quiet. That you seem so sad—"

"I am not sad," she said and burst into tears.

"Oh, crap," one male voice muttered, and then there was a general stampede and Jake, Caleb and Travis all tried to reach her at the same time.

Caleb got there first. He pulled her into his arms. She stood stiff, rigid, and then a sob broke from her throat and she fell against him, her tears soaking his flannel shirt.

"I'd like to get my hands on that prick," Travis said.

"Get in line," Jake said.

"He is *my* friend," Khan said. "*Was* my friend. I'm the one who gets first shot. To think he would turn into a man who would seduce a woman, convince her to be his mistress—"

"We seduced each other," Emily said.

Caleb shut his eyes. "Em. We don't need details."

"But it's true." She stepped out of her brother's arms, took her napkin from the table and blew her nose in it. "I wanted to sleep with Marco."

Jake grimaced. Travis ran his hands through his hair.

"And I wasn't his mistress. I worked for him. I was his PA. His AA. I was damned good at my job. I earned my pay legitimately, and I'm surprised that you would think I'd do anything less."

"I didn't," Jake said. "We didn't. It's just that—"

"When Laurel and I walked into that apartment and saw you, we were shocked. I had no idea—"

"I'm amazed," Emily said coldly, "you didn't fly straight here to tell my brothers what a—a fallen woman I'd become."

Khan rubbed his face with his hands.

"I had no wish to do that. Even when I realized that we had walked in just as Santini was ending your—your relationship. I told you, I would not have spoken of it but for what happened here today, what your family told me of your distress."

"I am not distressed! And he wasn't ending it." One lie out of two. Considering her average, that wasn't bad.

"Emily. I saw it with my own eyes. His coldness. His rage. He was in the middle of—of telling you that it was over when Laurel and I arrived."

"You're wrong. Everything was fine until you showed up."

"Great!" Travis shook his head, paced to the stove, then paced back. "It's your fault the SOB dumped her."

"I didn't mean it like that. Of course it wasn't Khan's fault." She ran the tip of her tongue over her bottom lip. "And he didn't dump me. Not the way you think. We were—we were in love."

"Until he got tired of you, the no-good—"

"No," Khan said.

They all looked at him. For the first time, he seemed uncertain.

Travis frowned. "What do you mean, no?"

"Laurel said it didn't make sense."

"A man taking advantage of our sister? Goddamned right, it doesn't make sense."

"Not that. What we saw... " Khan shook his head. "I spoke with Marco that afternoon. He invited us to dinner. I said I wanted him to meet Laurel. And he said that he wanted me to meet someone, too."

"So what?"

"So, why would he have wanted to introduce Emily to us if he were planning to end their relationship? It makes no sense but then, neither does the fact that the woman he said he wanted me to meet was named Emily Madison."

Silence.

The Wildes looked at him. At each other. And then, finally, at Emily.

"That's who he thought I was," she said in a small voice. "Emily Madison."

"Why?"

The word came from four throats. Emily gave a deep sigh.

"It's complicated."

The Wilde brothers and Khan folded their arms, the way Marco had always done when he was annoyed. Was it something arrogant men learned in in some secret ritual?

"It's true. I told him my name was Madison. Well, I'd told that to everybody. To every prospective employer. And—and, see, I live in a neighborhood that's not so great—"

"Not so great?" Travis said in a dangerous voice.

"It's what I can afford," Emily replied, her chin angling up. "It's difficult to make much money, playing piano in bars."

"Holy crap," Jake snarled. "Playing piano in—"

"That was how I met Marco. I'd been playing in a bar that was—that was kind of run down. And the owner fired me. And it was almost two in the morning and it was raining and I missed the bus and—"

Caleb made a sound that was more a snarl than anything else. Without thinking about it, Emily folded her arms. Her brothers were upset. She got that. But she'd be damned if she'd let them make easy judgments about the choices she'd made. Right or wrong, they'd been hers to make.

This was her life, not anyone else's.

"Here's the deal," she said. "You want to know what happened? Then try listening instead of playing judge and—"

The sound of an engine roared up outside. Good. The women were back. She might as well get this over with instead of having to tell the story twice.

Somebody knocked at the kitchen door.

"The girls must have forgotten their keys," Khan said.

"They don't need keys," Travis said. "They know that. The doors are never locked at *El Sueño*."

The knock came again. Harder. Much harder. Emily could almost see the door shake.

A strange feeling swept through her. A premonition. An awareness.

"Who in hell could that be?" Travis said tightly. "The last damn thing we want right now is visitors."

Jake strode to the door. Grasped the knob. Swung it open. It was dark outside; no moon, no stars.

"Yeah?" he said. "Who—"

Emily took a step forward.

"Marco?"

"Emily," that accented husky voice said, and he stepped through the door, the man she hated, the man she pitied, the man she had loved...

The man she would never stop loving.

Her Marco, dressed in jeans and a leather jacket, his hair a little too long, his face a little too thin, his eyes a little too haunted.

"Are you Marco Santini?" one of the Wilde brothers said.

*"Emilia mia,"* Marco said, his eyes on the woman he loved and had lost.

"Screw this," Jake growled, and Emily screamed, and that was the last thing Marco knew before a clean right uppercut connected with his jaw and he went down in a boneless heap.

****

"Marco. Marco, please, please speak to me! Marco groaned and opened his eyes. Where in hell was he? He was in a kitchen but not his big, blindingly white glass, steel and granite kitchen. This one had a Spanish tile floor, white stucco walls, a stove big enough to roast an ox.

He blinked. And looked into Emily's beautiful blue eyes. She was kneeling beside him and the sight of her filled his heart with joy.

"Emily," he whispered, "*cara mia.*"

"Talk English," a male voice growled.

He looked up. Four enormous men stood in a semicircle around Emily. Three of them looked alike. Big. Hard. Tough. Angry. The fourth was as big, as hard, as tough but not quite as angry. Was that…

"Khan? What are you—"

"What are *you* doing here, Santini?"

Marco switched his gaze to the man who had spoken.

"That's Travis," Emily whispered. "My brother."

Marco sat up. He touched his jaw and hissed through his teeth. His jaw hurt like hell.

"He asked you a question," the second man said.

"That's Jacob. My brother."

"Yeah. Answer the question," the third man growled.

"That's—"

"Caleb," Marco said. "*Si*. I figured that out for myself."

"Marco." It was Khan. "Listen, man, I hope you have some answers because I have to tell you, you are in enemy territory."

"I have answers."

"I sure as shit hope so," Jake Wilde snarled.

Marco ignored him. He had eyes only for Emily.

"I have missed you, *cara mia,*" he said softly. "More than you can ever know."

"Can that crap," Travis Wilde said.

"Yeah. Can it," Caleb Wilde said, "because you're not saying a word to Emily until you explain yourself to us."

A muscle knotted in Marco's cheek. Slowly, carefully, he got to his feet. The room tilted a little but he stood tall and straight as he looked from one Wilde brother to the next.

"I will explain myself to Emily first," he said quietly. "And then I will deal with the three of you." He looked at Emily. He wanted to take her in his arms but the look in her eyes told him nothing. Doing the correct thing next was important if he was to win her back. "I love you, *Emilia mia*."

"Are you deaf, dude? You need to face us before—"

"I love you with all my heart. With my soul. With all I have been, all I am, all I ever will be."

Emily's mouth trembled. With anger? Pain? Or with love?

"I loved you when I let you leave me. I never stopped loving you." He paused. He knew that what he said next would determine the rest of his life. "I was a fool, sweetheart. You did not lie to me, you lied to the world. About yourself, and why should you have done such a thing when you are the most brilliant, most beautiful woman any man has ever known?"

"Hey. Santini—"

"Shut up, Jacob," Emily said, very softly.

Jake's eyebrows shot up. He looked at his brothers. They shrugged their shoulders. After a second or two, so did he.

"It is the world's fault that you had to become Emily Madison, *cara*, because it was not wise enough to see that Emily Wilde was all that it needed. And then we met." He wanted to laugh but his throat felt too tight for laughter. "The most wonderful woman imaginable, and a man who is a stubborn fool. "

"You left out arrogant," Emily said. Her voice wobbled a little, just enough to give him hope. "A stubborn, arrogant fool."

"*Si*. I am both those things. But—"

"But," she said, her eyes locked to his, "I didn't mean to hurt you. I never, ever meant to do that."

"I know that, *inamorata*, just as I know that what you said that night was true. Emily Madison and Emily Wilde are the same woman. Being Emily Madison was all about what you needed, not about me." He took a step forward. She was so close now that he could smell the scent of her skin, of her hair. Carefully, he reached out, framed her face with his hands. "You were the first true thing in my entire life. And because of my selfish stupidity, I almost lost you."

Tears rolled down Emily's face. Her nose was running. Marco looked around; one of Emily's brothers—it would take him some time to connect their names to their faces—plucked a napkin from the table and handed it to him.

*"Grazie."*

"You're welcome," Caleb said, and he glared at his

brothers, daring them to say something, but neither of them did.

"*Cara.*" Gently, he dried her tears with the napkin, then wiped her nose. His heart was racing; he had closed hundreds of multi-million dollar business deals over the last several years and he had been cool and calm through all of them but this—this was not business. This was his life. "Sweetheart. Have I lost you? Tell me that I have not. Tell me that you understand that I am a stubborn, arrogant fool—but tell me that you forgive me."

Did seconds go by, or an eternity? Marco forgot to breathe. Then, slowly, the most beautiful smile in the world curved over his Emily's lips.

"At the very least," she said, "you're arrogant. But I love you. And I always will."

She went into his arms. He held her against him, his face buried in her hair. *"Emilia mia,"* he said brokenly, and she raised her face to his and he said her name again and kissed her.

Somebody shuffled his feet. Somebody cleared his throat. Somebody sniffled.

Marco let go of Emily, dug in the pocket of his jacket, found what he had never been without since the terrible night she had walked out of his life, and dropped to one knee.

"Emily Madison Wilde. Will you do me the honor of becoming my wife?"

He lifted his hand. The diamond-and-sapphire ring lay in the center of his palm, shining as brightly as the hope in his heart.

Emily gasped.

A chorus of masculine *wows* filled the air along with a counterpoint of feminine *oohs* because somewhere along the way the Wilde women and Laurel had come back.

"*Emilia mia. Per favore.* Will you marry me?"

Emily looked at the upturned face of her lover. She

could almost see the years stretching ahead, the two of them together, happy, in love, perhaps with babies to make their lives complete.

"Yes," she said softly, and she laughed. "Yes," she said, "yes, yes, yes—"

Marco Santini shot to his feet, gathered Emily Madison Wilde into his arms and kissed her.

And he did it to a round of welcoming applause.

# EPILOGUE

They were married on the winter solstice, at *El Sueño*.

Outside, a pristine white snow fell gently on the meadows and the distant hills. Fairy lights were wrapped along the corral railings and trailed up the front steps to the porch.

Inside, virtually all the townsfolk of Wilde's Crossing oohed and aahed over the beautiful bride and her handsome groom.

The general almost didn't get there in time—but he did, and he gave the bride away.

Lissa and Jaimie were both Emily's maids of honor; her sisters-in-law and Laurel were her bridesmaids. Her brothers were Marco's groomsmen and Khan was his best man.

"Made for each other," people whispered, and when Emily and Marco repeated the vows administered by Judge Arnold, who had known Emily all her life, some of the women sniffed back tears.

"They're right together," Jaimie told Lissa a couple of hours later, when they took a break from dancing by escaping to a corner of the big living room.

"They are," Lissa said. She looked at her sister. "You think it'll ever be like that for either of us, James?

A funny look swept over Jaimie's face but it happened so quickly that Lissa decided she'd imagined it.

"Not for me," she said, and Lissa grinned.

"Not for me, either. I mean, life's too full of choices, right?"

Jaimie nodded. "Sure," she said, and before Lissa could say anything else, Jaimie grabbed a pair of full champagne flutes from the tray carried by a passing waiter and handed one to her sister. *"Skoal,"* she said, "and *l'chaim* and *do svidanya*, or whatever it is you're supposed to say at a time like this."

The sisters knocked back the champagne. Then, laughing, they boogied out to the center of the dance floor.

A little while later, Emily went up the stairs to the loft.

"Here it comes," somebody yelled.

The drummer of the six-piece band that had kept everyone dancing all evening did a drumroll and Emily turned her back and tossed her bouquet over her head.

Jaimie was the only single woman who didn't cheer and jump up to try to snag the flowers and yet, with unerring accuracy, they came straight at her.

"Catch it," somebody yelled.

Purely on instinct, she did. She stared at the baby pink and white orchids for a long minute and then she gave a dramatic shudder and pushed the flowers into Lissa's hands while all the guests laughed.

Upstairs, Emily changed into a pale blue cashmere dress and an ankle length, sapphire-blue cashmere coat. Marco changed into khakis, a dark blue shirt and his leather bomber jacket. He was on his way down when the Wilde brothers and Khan caught up to him.

"So," Travis said gruffly, "you married Em."

He grinned. "Damned right I did."

"She's one hell of a lady," Caleb said.

Marco nodded. He could see where this was going.

"You'll remember to treat her right," Jacob said.

Khan didn't say anything. He just stood there, arms folded, a determined expression on his face.

Marco looked them over, his eyes meeting and holding the eyes of each man.

"Here's the deal," he said quietly, the phrase so properly American that only his slight accent gave him away. "I adore Emily. I will always adore her. I will care for her and protect her and make her happy every day of our lives." His mouth flattened. "But if any one of you goons ever lays a hand on me again, I'll show you exactly what it means to have been born in Sicily." He looked into the eyes of each of them again. *"Capisci?"*

His new brothers and his old friend grinned.

"Got it," they said, and they all shook hands and slapped each other on the back and, what the hell, ended up exchanging bear hugs because from now on, they were a family.

****

The newlyweds flew to New York on Marco's plane.

The flight wasn't long enough. How could it be when there was a private bedroom where they could spend the hours in each other's arms?

Charles met them at the airport. He smiled, shook Marco's hand, started to shake Emily's hand as well, but she laughed and kissed him.

A light, lovely snow was falling as they drove through the streets of Manhattan.

"I love the city when it's like this," Emily said softly as she sat within the curve of her husband's arm. "It's so beautiful."

"Beautiful," he said solemnly, and tilted her face to his for a kiss.

The doorman greeted them with a smile.

"Welcome home, Mrs. Santini, Mr. Santini. Congratulations."

They rode up to the penthouse, their arms around each other, Emily's head on Marco's shoulder. When the elevator doors opened, Marco said, "Wait, *cara.*" He stepped out, hit the switch and the entire foyer and huge living room blazed with light.

Emily clapped her hands in delight.

There were flowers everywhere. Orchids. Roses.

Mums. Lilies. But that wasn't the reason for her gasp, or for the way her hands flew to her heart.

At the far end of the living room, framed by the floor-to-ceiling windows, a grand piano waited for its new owner.

"My wedding gift, *cara,*" Marco said. He hesitated. His wife had not moved. She had not spoken. Had he made a mistake?

*"Emilia mia.* What is it?"

She shook her head. She was weeping; how could she speak when her heart was so full?

"Emily. Please…"

She looked at her husband. "How did you know?" she whispered. "How did you guess? It's—it's like having a missing piece of me come back."

Marco grinned. "You like it, huh?"

He looked arrogant as hell and so incredibly gorgeous that she had no choice but to fly into his arms.

"It's the best gift in the world!"

He took her hand as they walked through the room. When they reached the piano, she reached out a hand and stroked her fingers over the beautiful black surface.

"Do you realize that I have never heard you play?"

She nodded. "I know."

"Will you play for me now, sweetheart?"

She hesitated. Then she down on the piano bench, flexed her fingers, put her hands on the keys…

And played.

Not Sinatra. Not Billy Joel. Not any of the songs she'd played at the Tune-In.

She played Beethoven's "Für Elise." DeFalla's "Ritual Fire Dance." And then, because it was her favorite and she had not dared to attempt it in years, Chopin's "Fantaisie Impromptu."

When the last notes had died away, Marco was almost afraid to speak. Then he whispered his wife's name and she rose from the bench and he gathered her into his arms and held her close.

"You are not a piano player," he said, after a long, long time. "You are a pianist."

Her could feel her lips curve in a smile against his throat, even as he felt the warmth of her tears.

"My father never thought so. When I was little and people would say, 'What do you want to be when you grow up, Emily?' I'd say that I wanted to be a pianist. And he'd laugh, but in a way I'm sure he thought was kind, and he'd say, 'Emily's always going to be our little piano player.'"

Marco drew back. He looked into Emily's eyes and thought what a miracle it was that he had found everything a man could ever need or want in this one amazing woman.

"You are capable of being whatever you wish to be, *Emilia mia.*"

She knew that he meant it. And, for the first time in her life, she knew that it was true. She was who she was, Emily Madison Wilde Santini, and life held endless possibilities.

And one great, sustaining truth.

"Yes, sweetheart," she said softly, "but most of all, what I want to be is your wife."

Marco's eyes darkened as he swept her up into his arms.

"That is a very good thing," he said, "because what I want, most of all, is to be your husband."

And as the snow fell over the city and turned it into a place of magic and wonder, the man who had never needed anyone carried his bride to their bedroom to begin their new life.

Together.

## Coming Next

**Books Two & Three**
**The Wilde Sisters**

***JAIMIE: FIRE & ICE***
***LISSA: SUGAR & SPICE***

Made in the USA
Lexington, KY
19 July 2013